ALSO BY HELEN FROST

When
My Sister
Started
Kissing

When My Sister Started Kissing

HELEN FROST

MARGARET FERGUSON BOOKS

FARRAR STRAUS GIROUX · NEW YORK

Farrar Straus Giroux Books for Young Readers
An imprint of Macmillan Publishing Group, LLC
175 Fifth Avenue, New York 10010

Copyright © 2017 by Helen Frost
All rights reserved
Printed in the United States of America
Designed by Elizabeth H. Clark
First edition, 2017

3 5 7 9 10 8 6 4 2

mackids.com

Library of Congress Cataloging-in-Publication Data

Names: Frost, Helen, 1949– author.
Title: When my sister started kissing / Helen Frost.
Description: First edition. | New York : Farrar Straus Giroux, 2017. | "Margaret Ferguson Books." | Summary: Claire and Abi have always loved summers at the lake house, but a pregnant stepmother and Abi's intense new interest in boys have changed everything.
Identifiers: LCCN 2016028011 (print) | LCCN 2016054982 (ebook) | ISBN 9780374303037 (hardback) | ISBN 9780374303044 (Ebook)
Subjects: | CYAC: Novels in verse. | Sisters—Fiction. | Dating (Social customs)—Fiction. | Stepmothers—Fiction. | Lakes—Fiction. | BISAC: JUVENILE FICTION / Family / Siblings. | JUVENILE FICTION / Social Issues / New Experience.
Classification: LCC PZ.5.F76 Whe 2017 (print) | LCC PZ.5.F76 (ebook) | DDC [Fic]—dc23
LC record available at https://lccn.loc.gov/2016028011

Our books may be purchased in bulk for promotional, educational, or business use. Please contact your local bookseller or the Macmillan Corporate and Premium Sales Department at (800) 221-7945 ext. 5442 or by e-mail at MacmillanSpecialMarkets@macmillan.com.

Dedicated to these lakes I have loved
Lake Kabekona
Spec Pond
Lake Ossipee
Loch Mannoch
xx
and to Chad
xx

When My Sister Started Kissing

You Make Me Happy
    Heartstone Lake remembers

The baby, Claire, in a sunsuit and
yellow hat, sat on her father's shoulders, the
great wide world spread out before them. Two
egrets flew home to their nest as thunder
rumbled, far off in the distance.

The mother, Cari, lifted Abigail—
You are my sunshine, they sang together,
gently rocking. Cari waded in up to her ankles.
Everyone was smiling then, held close by the
rhythm of the song: *You make me happy.*

Blue sky, one cloud, an open beach
umbrella shading their red blanket. Did the
raindrops fall from the sun itself? I remember
no cold wind, no whitecaps, just a few small
indentations on my glassy surface,
not enough to make them pack up and
go home. Cari smiled at her husband, Andrew, and at

Baby Claire, who whimpered. I did not know why. Did she
realize, before the others did, what was coming, what it meant?
It seemed to happen all at once: Claire cried out, the sky
grew dark, lightning sent its dazzle through me. Cari
held Abigail tight in her arms for a split second,
then fell, her face in mine.

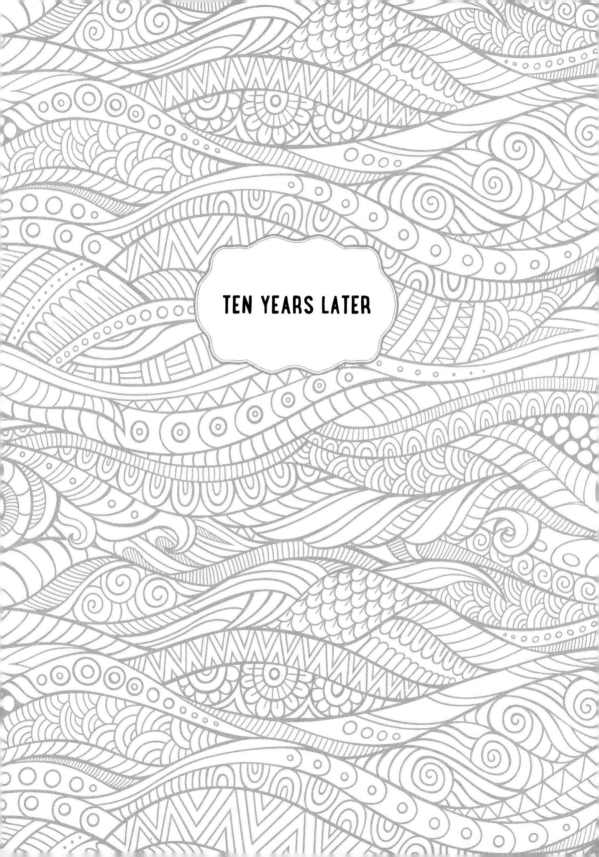

TEN YEARS LATER

Wishing
Claire

Dad glances in the rearview mirror. *Get ready,* he says,
to make your wish. We're about to cross the railroad track.
We've turned off the highway onto the gravel road
that circles Heartstone Lake. Abigail smiles back

at Dad, lifts her feet. *We always do this,* she explains
to Pam, who says, *That's a nice family tradition.*
Dad doesn't even have to think about his wish.
He says what he says every year: *Good fishing!*

He winks. Abigail and I exchange a look. We love
Dad, but when we're at the lake, fishing is all
he ever thinks about. Pam has something else
on her mind: *I wish we could decide what to call*

the baby. She looks at Dad, then out the window.
If she's thinking up a nature name like Buck,
she doesn't tell him—or us. Abigail's distracted,
trying to get a signal on her phone. No luck.

Tell me again how long we'll be here, Dad? she says.
About a month, he says. *We always have the landline.*

She tries again, gives up, turns to me. *What's your
wish?* she asks. I shrug and peer into the trees, trying

to see the lake. Every year when I was little, I'd lift
my feet and wish for the same thing: *To see Mom again.*
Last year, I closed my eyes and thought: *I wish Dad would
not get married.* I knew it was impossible. And mean.

I hated Pam already. Her makeup and nail polish,
all those different-colored shoes and fancy jewelry.
I wished we could keep our cabin for the three of us,
like it had always been—just Dad and Abigail and me.

It halfway worked. Pam didn't come to the lake
with us last year. So that wish came true. Sort
of—in September, they got married as they'd planned.
And this morning we all got in the car, heading north.

This year, I've decided to change my wishing strategy
to something more realistic: I know Pam is here to stay,
but I wish she'd quit trying so hard to be our mom.
The cabin's small. It won't be easy to stay out of her way.

I look across the backseat at Abigail. Sun shines
through her brown curls. Whatever she's wishing
sends color to her cheeks, and her half smile says
she has a secret. I bet her wish is about kissing.

Memories
  Abigail

Claire was just a baby. She can't remember
    the day Mom died. And I can't forget—even
        if I wanted to. I have a lightning-shaped scar

on my arm, reminding me of that rain and thunder
    and lightning. All of us crying except Mom, who
        did not cry. Or talk. Or move. We had to leave

her on our blanket on the beach. Dad
    carried Claire, and I walked in front of them
        up the path to the cabin. We got in the car,

and Dad drove down the road to the Johnsons'.
    TJ was three years old, like I was. He gave me
        Benjamin Bunny, his stuffed rabbit, so I wouldn't cry.

Dad promised him we'd give it back, but I
    refused to let that bunny go. Each year, I'd think,
        This summer, I'll give him back to TJ. And then

I somehow wouldn't. By now, it would seem
    so childish to give him back. Especially after
        what happened the night before we left last summer.

Puzzle Pieces
  Claire

We're almost there. I love the pine-tree
smell as we get close. It makes me feel like
I belong here. Just one of many things I love:
Sunsets reflected on the water. Riding my bike

over gravel roads. A light breeze blowing
through my hair when I'm out in the kayak.
Loons and swans and water lilies. Dad met Mom
when they worked at a camp across the lake, back

when they were teenagers. They fell in love,
got married, and came here for a month each year.
They planned their lives around it—Dad became
an English teacher so they could be here

every summer. He tells us how much Mom loved this
cabin, and we've kept things like they were. Our book-
shelves are full of her poetry and art books—some
with corners still turned back so we can look

for the pages she was reading. Her easel stands
by the window, holding her watercolor of a birch

tree with a bluebird in it. That tree was half as tall
back then, compared to now. Bluebirds still perch

on the branches—do great-grandchildren
of the one Mom painted fly past our trees?
When we're at the cabin, I like to think:
Mom picked up this exact same puzzle piece

and fit it in its place. Or: *She got out of jail free*
with this Monopoly card—and now so can I.
Her parents built the cabin the year she turned
eleven—the age I'll be by the time we leave. I try

to picture her and Dad building the new addition
the year I was a baby—the year Mom died.
I've heard about that all my life: how Dad
set me down and ran into the water. He tried

to save Mom, but he couldn't. He could only save Abigail
and me. All three of us must have been so scared.
Now we're almost to the cabin. I won't say this out loud,
but being here with Pam is going to be a little weird.

Almost the Same, Except
Claire

The minute Dad unlocks the door, and we
go in, I'm like— Whoa! What happened here?
Everything is almost the same, except—
I don't know—I shake my head to clear

my thoughts. When Dad and Pam drove up last
weekend, Abigail and I would have come, too,
but our cousin invited us to a roller-skating
party, and we stayed home so we could go.

When they got back, Dad said, *We changed
some things around,* and we were like, *Sure. That
sounds good.* (I didn't mind missing out on sweeping
up the mouse poop.) But this is way more than what

he prepared us for: Everything straightened up. Puzzles
and games moved to a top shelf, leaving the game shelf
empty—except for a flower vase. My throat tightens.
That vase—I bet it's Pam's. I make myself

stay quiet. Dad says, *Girls, let's get the car unpacked.
Pam shouldn't carry anything too heavy. Claire,*

can you get the fishing poles and tackle box?
Abigail, you can set the cooler over there.

He points toward an empty space
under the window—where Mom's easel
used to be. Where did they put it?
And where's her chair? Deep and cozy,

my favorite place to sit and read the books I love
(where are the books?) or watch a storm roll across
the water—I felt like that chair could hug me.
Abigail looks like she did when she lost

her sketchbook one day last summer
after we'd spent all day at the beach,
and then she found it a week later,
off a trail where she had to reach

into poison ivy to retrieve it. *Dad,*
I manage, *where's Mom's . . . chair?*
I catch a look between him and Pam.
Dad says, *Remember? The back of it had a tear*

in the cloth. And, he adds, *we'll need that space*
pretty soon now, for the baby. That word—*we*—
slides by so easily, erasing my word—*Mom.*
I wonder—does it erase Abigail and me?

All Mom's Art
Claire

I get it. I do. All the stuff from our old life together
would make Pam feel like she does not belong.
This rearrangement says: *Pam is here to stay. And
make room for the baby.* Don't get me wrong,

I know it's not the baby's fault. He's not even born yet.
But—over there? I nudge Abigail and nod to where all
our framed pictures—even that cheesy one of the four
of us in bright green shirts—aren't hanging on the wall.

Plus . . . *Look,* I whisper. Abigail sucks air through her nose.
All Mom's art—and ours—has disappeared. Dad's gone
back to the car. Pam stares out the window, blocking the light,
resting her hands on her stomach as she stands there, alone.

Cough, Sputter, Blink
Claire

Dad has this little thing he does—
half cough, half sputter, a little blink,
before he answers one of our tough
questions. But really? I wouldn't think

something like this would throw him off.
This morning, Abigail, standing with her back
to me as she got dressed, said in a quiet voice,
Claire, I think I need a bra. News flash—

she's thirteen. I said, *Tell Dad,* and she said, *I will.*
Now the two of them are doing the supper dishes,
and she tells him. I expect him to go, *Blah, blah, blah,*
my little girl is growing up. But Dad actually blushes

and looks down at the dishwater. *I'm not sure I'm*
the one to help with that, he says, with a glance across
the room at Pam, who jumps right in like she
knows Abigail better than Dad does, and of course

she is now our family expert on girls' clothes.
I'd be happy to take you shopping. Let's go soon,

before the baby is born, she says. Abigail glances
at me. Pam says, *How about tomorrow afternoon?*

I'm sure Abigail will hate this, but the look
she gives me seems to mean, *How can I say no?*
Before I know it, Pam has the whole thing
planned, and Abigail has agreed to go.

Just the two of them. I'm not jealous. I don't
like the mall. But seriously, Dad? Please.
Finding new underwear for Abigail is harder
than patching up a couple hundred skinned knees?

Splinting my broken ankle, halfway up that mountain?
Harder than selling Girl Scout cookies in a blizzard?
Taking your daughter shopping is suddenly harder
than burying Stokie, our three-year-old pet lizard?

Harder
than burying
Mom?
I don't want to start crying.

I'm going out in the kayak, I say.
Dad knows I won't be gone too long.
But Pam butts in and tries to tell me
what time I should come home.

Sunset

Claire, in the kayak

Out in the kayak at **sunset**,

     water bugs walk **across**

          orange light on **the water**.

              What if Pam **offers me**

                    a trip to town? Shopping **time**

              has always meant Dad-time **to**

         me. Pam doesn't have to **be**

     our mom! I like being **alone**

with Dad—and **with myself**.

Welcome Back
The lake

She stood on the shore looking
out. Now, in the kayak, she moves across
my surface through the water lilies, observing
every water bug, each jumping fish, following the
birds through air and water. Two loons call to each
other—or do they call to Claire? She watches them
dive, tries to guess where they'll come up. Every
year when the family arrives, she greets me

like a good friend, wearing a pair of
old jeans, a faded sweatshirt under her life
vest. Sometimes a baseball cap, tilted sideways.
Everything well worn, comfortable. She always
seems to need a haircut—her shaggy bangs

(uncut for how long?) hang over her eyes
so she has to keep pushing them back

all the time. She started out taking
long, hard strokes. Now she
leans back to rest.

Come On In
    Claire

Let's go swimming, Abigail suggests.
It's our second morning here; the lake is clear
and cool. A school of minnows skims across
the rocky bottom. *Come on, Claire, over here!*

she says as she dives off the dock. Out on the lake,
two ducks glide in for a landing. Abigail turns
to me, laughing. *It's not so cold,* she calls out,
once you get used to it. My stomach churns

as I go in slowly, step-by-tiny-step,
dipping my toes, my knees, into the shallow
part, until I'm in up to my waist. Abigail,
already past the drop-off, dares me to follow.

She swims straight out to where the current
carries her toward Anna's Island. Water flows
from one end of the lake to the other, and near
the island the current helps a swimmer who knows

how to catch it. That's fun—you can swim faster
than you thought you could. Of course,

if you try to swim against that current, instead of
being a better swimmer than usual, you're worse.

Once at the end of last summer, Abigail and I swam
out to the island, and Dad rowed his boat beside me
to give me a ride back. This year, will I be able
to swim all the way out and back? We'll see.

Splashing It with Color
  Abigail

I've been told I was a happy baby,
    a cheerful little girl. I'd wake up,
        jump out of bed, and Mom would say,

Good morning, sweet Abigail. According to Dad,
    she and I lit up the room together. *Every morning,*
        like the crack of dawn, he says, *she was the lake—*

dark, still, and quiet. You were the sun
    splashing it with color. How does that
        make Claire feel? I don't know. Was she

fast asleep those early mornings
    when all that Mom-and-me joy
        opened the day? We've shared

a room since Claire was born, so I know she must
    have been there. Has she always liked to let the sun
        begin its climb into the sky before she opens up her eyes?

Would You Be Okay?
Claire

I'm taking the boat to the marina this morning, Dad says.
Who wants to come? I love being on the lake with Dad. *I do!*
I say. *And when we get back, I want to go over to the Johnsons'.*
Abigail, if you're back from the mall by then, you should come, too.

TJ and the little kids will want to see you. Before Abigail
says yes or no, Pam says, *We might not be back from town*
until late afternoon. Do you still want to go? Abigail says,
Yes. And then, to me, *You can go to the Johnsons' on your own.*

Pam asks how far away the Johnsons live, and Dad says,
Our nearest neighbors—just up the road. Abigail is sure: she
would rather go with Pam than go to their house. That look
flits across her face—something she isn't telling me.

If She Knew
Abigail

What would Claire say if she knew that TJ and I

       kissed, the night before we left last summer?

              And—what does TJ think about that now?

We were talking, and admitted that we wondered

       what kissing is like. I said, *We could try it,* and TJ said,

              Why not? We agreed: it was fun! But how will it feel

to see him again now? Since he lives here in no-phone-land,

       we haven't even texted since that day. Will it be awkward

              if we end up alone together? Although that shouldn't be

too hard to avoid, with all those little spies in his house—

       especially the nosy twins. Not sure which one it was who

              caught us holding hands behind their boathouse, a minute

after we had kissed, and blurted out, *I'm telling!*

       TJ thought fast. *Nothing to tell,* he told her. *Abigail*

              tripped, and I helped her up. That's it. Now scram.

Dad's Hand on the Tiller
Claire

Good—since Abigail isn't going to the marina,
I have Dad all to myself. The water's rough
and he goes pretty fast, making me laugh as we
go bumping over the waves. It's enough

just being together—we don't try to talk over
the motor, but we point things out to each other:
three turtles lined up on a log, a pair of swans
at the entrance to the channel leading to another

lake, a blue dragonfly that lands on Dad's hand
as he holds the tiller. At the marina, he buys bait
and gasses up the boat. I get an ice cream sandwich,
and go out on the dock to eat it while I wait

for him to talk to everyone he hasn't seen all year.
We ran into Fred and Ruth Gibson: this could take
a while. They like to know—and tell—everything
about everyone, all up and down our side of the lake.

As we head back home, Dad says he heard
about a new fishing spot he wants to try out.

We drop our anchor there, and I sit quietly
with him while he casts for perch and trout.

After a while, he asks me to pick up the oars
and row over to a slightly different spot.
He's not catching much, but we stay here for
an hour or so. Comfortable, talking a little—or not.

The Lake Trail
Claire

Someone has already cleared the lake trail
to the Johnsons' house, so I walk
along it, and find TJ all by himself,
fishing from the end of their dock.

Hi, Claire, he says. *When did you get here?*
I saw your dad and—what's her name? Ann?—
last week, but I didn't have a chance to ask when you
were coming. He tosses a small fish back in.

We got here on Sunday, I say. *Her name is Pam.*
She's about to have a baby. He laughs. *Moms do that a lot.*
Well, his does, that's true—she has three kids
younger than me. But I remind TJ, *Pam's not*

our mom. I dangle my feet from the side of the dock,
staying quiet so I don't scare away the fish.
I've always liked TJ. He's nice to me, and
never treats me like a little kid. I wish

I had him for a brother. One time, the summer
before last, he fixed Abigail's bike, and I told her

she should marry him. She laughed at me, but TJ
smiled in a nice way—not like he was so much older.

He reels in a fish, catches it in his landing net. *A good-sized*
walleye. Second one this morning. You guys want it? he asks.
He even says, *I'll clean it for you.* Three mallard
ducks swim under the dock, then go on past.

TJ's sisters and brother come down to the dock.
Sadie's hair is longer than Sophia's this year.
We're six now, Sophia brags. Devon adds, *I'm nine.*
I found my own way down here. He smiles ear to ear

about the handrail that TJ and Mr. Johnson built
for him, since he only sees a tiny bit, out of one eye.
I hug all of them. TJ wraps the fish in newspaper
and gives it to me, saying, *Tell your sister I said hi.*

Mirror
Claire

Abigail and Pam are back. I count seven
shopping bags. We've never worn anything
but old jeans and T-shirts up here at the cabin,
and now Abigail is pulling out new running

clothes, new shoes, and all these shorts and tops.
She got a haircut, and gold highlights in her hair.
Plus something weird happened to her eyebrows.
I don't know when she started to care

about all this. She models a white swimsuit,
an expensive kind with sleeves. *Pam agreed*
it was worth it, she says. *Now I won't wear a shirt*
to cover up my lightning scar, and I won't need

as much sunscreen when we go to the beach.
That's true, I guess. *Abigail,* I say, *that scar*
has faded so much you can hardly see it now.
She studies her arm in the mirror. *Are*

you sure? she asks. *Yes, I am. No one will notice*
it. She says, *Thanks,* and smiles at the mirror

(it agrees: she's cute), then looks at me
and squints one eye, to see if I share her

admiration. I look out the window. *Claire,*
she asks, *are you upset because Pam and I*
went shopping? No. It doesn't bother me—
it's just so stupid. *Of course not,* I say. *Why*

would I be? I can hate Pam all by myself—I don't need
your help. Abigail tilts her head. *Pam's not so bad,*
she says. *Give her a chance.* Whatever. Let
the two of them be girlfriends—I still have Dad.

Glitter and Gloss
Claire

Abigail comes to supper with glittery eyelids,
glossy pink lips, plus the gold streaks in her hair.
Pam does this thing where she catches Dad's
eye with a meaningful glance: *Don't go there,*

don't say what you're thinking, it warns him.
He gives a slight nod, then, *Claire,* he
says instead, *remember to put your bike away—*
it might rain. I answer, *Okay, Dad,* and we

all go back to trying not to stare at Abigail. Pam
decides this would be a good time to call
attention to a stain on my T-shirt, and says in a
bright voice, *They're having a sale at the mall*

all this week. I'd be happy to take you to get some new
summer clothes. And maybe, she has to add, *Chloe*
could fix your hair a little bit. Get your bangs
out of your eyes? She thinks I'm ugly

and unfashionable. I bet she assumes
I'm jealous of my sister. Guess what? None

of that is true. *No thanks,* I say. I don't want to be the kind of girl I bet Pam was, when she was one.

Eastside Swimming Beach
Claire

I wouldn't mind staying home today, but it
sounds like Abigail wants to wear her new
clothes where someone besides us will see them.
I'm tired of the cabin, she says. *What should we do?*

So after lunch, we pump up our bike tires
and head down the gravel road. We pass TJ's
house—he's out working on the motor
for their boat, and looks up when he sees

me wave to him. *Hi, Abigail,* he calls out. Why
does she just speed past and ride on? We steer
around the dog that always chases us—
either it's slower or we're faster this year.

Then we pedal by the gravel pit and boat launch,
coast past Loon Landing (a big house some rich
guy built two years ago), and now here we are
at the old familiar Eastside Swimming Beach.

Everything is the same as always—music blasting;
the smell of sunscreen; the flagpole a little bent;

band kids selling snacks at the concession
stand, which still needs a coat of paint;

a group of moms watching toddlers play in the sand;
a few old people. I wonder if anyone I know is here.
There's a group of kids who live here year-round, but
Jonilet isn't with them—she was my best friend last year.

Abigail and I park our bikes and head toward the spot
where we always spread our blanket, part shade,
part sun. She likes to sit and sketch after we swim.
I usually watch people, or take out a book and read.

What Is Summer For?
Abigail

There are always lots of boys here
      at the lake, and what is summer for?
            Fun. That's what. It looks like Michael,

from last summer, is the lifeguard. Brock Sundet
      might be here—not that he'd notice me, but . . .
            Wait, is that him going over to talk to Michael?

Claire, I say, *let's put our blanket over there*
      near that girl braiding that other girl's hair.
            See them? Right in front of the lifeguard stand.

Something's Different
Claire

Abigail spreads her stuff out on our blanket,
slathers her face and legs with sunscreen,
kicks off her flip-flops, and runs into the water.
I stand on the shore and watch her become queen

of Eastside Beach. She dives under the rope,
comes up laughing, flings water from her hair
into a ring of sunlight, attracting a swarm
of boys—were they even here last year?

I know they were. But something's different now.
Last summer, Abigail liked to look at boys—
a lot—this year, the boys are looking back. She's like
a kid on Christmas morning with a pile of new toys.

Pointers
Claire

At times, it seems like Abigail is still the same
as she's always been. When we got back
from the beach today, we came into our room
and stretched out on our beds to relax.

Pam has this blog called "Pointers from Pam."
Little tips about how to get extra use out of all
the things normal people throw away, like
the cardboard tube inside a toilet-paper roll:

"Cut one up and paint it to make napkin rings!
Use them to keep your socks in pairs!" Umm . . .
really? Would anyone actually do that? Abigail
and I try not to laugh at something that dumb,

but sometimes in private we make up pointers
of our own: "If your parents won't let you do
something you want to do, try asking when they're
too busy to say no." And: "They might believe you

if you tell one of them the other one said yes."
Even though I'm not quite eleven, we call ours "Tips

for Teens." But today when I say, *I have a tip for teens,*
Abigail walks over to the mirror to gloss her lips,

kisses a piece of Kleenex, then kisses the air and
announces, *I'm not going to make fun of Pam anymore.*
What? One trip to the mall, a haircut, a new swimsuit,
and now she's on Pam's side? *Wow, Abigail,* I say, *how mature.*

All I Did
Abigail

God, Claire, quit looking at me like
        you think I'm some kind of traitor
               to our childhood. All I did was

get a few new clothes and let a girl
        named Chloe cut and tint my hair.
               Don't act like you don't know me.

Well, okay, yes, we also went
        to the eyebrow place—you have
               eyebrows, too, somewhere under

those two caterpillars on your face.
        I'm not trying to be mean. It's just—
               I'm a girl. I like to look like one, okay?

Dad's Still Dad

Claire

Are you still mad at me?

It's just that—
everything's different this year.

I remember. You, me, and
Benjamin Bunny, all zipped up
in one sleeping bag.

Are you ever going to give that rabbit
back to TJ?

Maybe you could do that for yourself.

Or maybe not.

Abigail

Not mad. Maybe a little annoyed.
But never mind.

Not everything. Dad's still Dad.
Remember that time when we were little,
and he put up the tent
so we could sleep outside,
and then we got scared, but we still
wanted to sleep in the tent,
so he let us bring the whole
tent into the cabin?

Yeah.

I don't know.
Maybe you could do that for me?

TJ has probably forgotten about him.

Claire	Abigail
	You could take Benjamin Bunny over there, and give him to Sadie and Sophia.
It seems like you're avoiding TJ.	
	No I'm not! It's just that . . .
	I don't know. It's hard to explain.
Dad, is that you at the door?	

Dad

Are you girls still awake?

Claire	Abigail
Yes.	*Come on in.*

Dad

Want me to play my banjo while you go to sleep?

Claire	Abigail
Sure, Dad.	*Like you always used to.*

My Side of the Blanket
Claire

Today is too hot to ride bikes to the beach,
so we take the canoe, staying close
to the edge of the lake where the trees
hang over the water. A breeze cools us

as we paddle past the sandbar, through
the water lilies, past Anna's Island. We pull
the canoe onto Eastside Beach and pick the same
spot as yesterday for our blanket. Abigail

stretches out in the sun while I go get a drink,
and just as I return, a boy walks by and
says, *Hey.* Abigail looks up at him, smiles as if
they're friends, and answers, *Hi.* She brushes sand

off my side of the blanket. He says, *I'm Brock,* and then
this happens: *I'm Abi,* says Abigail. What's that
about? When did my sister change her name
from Abigail to Abi? Brock takes off his Cubs cap

and sits down like he's some famous person
who doesn't have to ask if anyone would mind.

"Abi" sees me standing there and gives a
subtle sign that means: *Claire, could you find*

something else to do for a while? Go for a swim?
Come back later? If we had our bikes instead
of the canoe, I'd just go home right now.
This boy, Brock, can have the stupid

blanket. But I can't leave "Abi" stranded here.
I walk away slowly, listening to them talk.
He asks, *Here for the summer?* She says, *We come up*
for about a month every year. How about you? Brock

says, *We stay here all summer.* Abi: *You're lucky.*
I wish we did. When did my sister learn this
whole new talking-to-boys voice? She sounds like
she got a part in a play and this is the first practice.

Jonilet
Claire

Good—Jonilet is here today. *Hi, Claire,* she says.
She gestures toward Abigail: *Your sister*
looks different this year. Sit with me? Is it that
obvious? With Brock and "Abi" sitting together

on our blanket, I don't know what to do
or where to go, and that must be clear
to Jonilet. She's going into sixth grade
like I am, but she also looks different this year—

more like a teenager. She got her braces off.
Her hair is curly. And, wow, her hands—with
all different-colored fingernails, and a fancy
henna tattoo going up around her wrist.

We walk past my blanket. "Abi" doesn't
look up when I go by, but I can see
her cheeks are burning, either from the sun
or from sitting so close to a boy. Jonilet says, *He*

likes her. His name is Brock Sundet—I know him.
This summer he's been coming to the beach

every day. Which seems to make a lot of these
girls happy. One day last week, he got a leech

stuck to his ankle, and all those girls over there had
ideas about how to get it off. Everyone seemed to enjoy
the drama. You know? No, I don't know.
I sure wouldn't want to get a leech off a boy.

These Two Sisters
    The lake

Listen to these two, paddling home
    in their canoe, quiet at first, then a little
eruption of argument, another space of quiet.

Birds fly overhead and come to rest on the water
as the conversation begins again. *So what if he is*
    cute, Abigail—I'm just asking what else you
        know about him. That's Claire.

    Abigail replies, *Could you call me Abi from*
    now on? Claire scowls, paddles harder. *Why? I*
    don't see what's wrong with "Abigail," she says.

That's what we've always called you. A fish jumps
high in the air. Abi says, *I've outgrown that name.*
    End of that question for now. Back to Brock:

    Sometimes you just know things, Abi says.
Even though we just met, I can tell he's nice. Plus,
    all those girls who keep looking at him can't be

45

wrong, can they? Abi smiles. Claire
is unimpressed. *He lives near that house they call*
Loon Landing, says Abi, paddling more slowly,
looking in that direction. *I remember seeing*

him at the beach last year, but we never met, she says.
Oh, is all Claire answers. Abi says, *I don't know, I just*
like him—and by the way, you don't have to go blabbing to
Dad about this. Claire asks, *Why not?* then adds, *Maybe*

you should be the one to say something . . . Abi. But Abi
only smiles as they paddle on toward home,
under hanging branches, into deep water.

New Running Clothes
Claire

Abigail—Abi—has always liked to get up early
when we're at the lake, to go for a sunrise swim.
Last summer, she'd swim to Anna's Island and back.
Not me. When we're up here, I like to sleep in.

But this morning, I open my eyes just enough
to see her put on her new running clothes.
The lake is rough today, she tells me. *I think I'll go
for a run instead. I'll leave a note for Dad.* She goes

out, and two hours later Dad and I, and Pam,
are having breakfast, when Abi comes in, all smiles.
Dad says, *Thanks for your note. Why is it signed "Abi"?*
She says, *Can you call me that now? I ran five miles—*

*first, down the road past Loon Landing, where I saw
someone I know from the beach, and we ran together,
all the way to the general store. We stopped for
a smoothie and I jogged back here. The weather*

doesn't look too good for fishing today, Dad.
That was clever, switching the conversation

over to fishing before Dad asks which friend
she ran into, or comes up with another question

about her name change. Do he and Pam notice that
Abi curled her hair and put makeup on her face
before she went out running? *You look happy, Abi,*
is all Pam says. *I can tell you love this place.*

Wind at Our Back
Claire

Whitecaps on the lake today, too rough
for the canoe. A good day to stay inside and read,
if you ask me, but Abi wants to go to the beach.
We could ride our bikes, she says. She doesn't need

me to go along—she could go by herself and see
who's there. But she keeps insisting,
*Claire, you come, too. What if I don't know
anyone there today, and I'm stuck sitting*

all by myself? Right. That would be a problem.
I know what you mean, I say. I could remind
her why I know, but I let it go, and bring a blanket
of my own. We go fast on the way there, the wind

at our backs—it will be harder on the way home.
When we get to the beach, I look around. Brock
is at the concession stand, that group of girls
sitting together nearby. They look up as we walk

past. *Sit with us,* a girl says to Abi. She answers,
Thanks, and spreads her blanket beside theirs.

They were talking to her, and not to me. What
should I do? I don't think my sister cares

where I sit, as long as it's not with her. The
girls are talking to Abi now. I see them look
over her shoulder at Brock and two other boys
walking toward them. I'm glad I brought a book.

I find a place to sit in the shade and read.
I look around for Jonilet, but I don't see
her or anyone else I know. Brock is sitting beside
Abi now. I'm sure she's not thinking about me.

A Little Bit Closer
Abi

I like this boy, Brock, and I think he likes me.
    When he says something funny he glances
        at me, and if I laugh, he inches a little bit closer.

What if he's thinking about kissing me? I'm not sure
    I really know how to kiss. I've only kissed that one time
        last summer. I wonder how many times Brock has kissed.

We Rest, Swim On
Claire

Wake up, Claire, it's the Fourth of July! Abi says.
Want to swim to the island with me? The lake
is calm today. I could swim out there, but home,
with the current against me? Probably not. *I'll take*

the kayak. You swim and I'll go beside you, I say. Abi says,
You made it out there one time last summer. I bet
you can swim back by now. I'll ask Dad if it's okay.
Dad says, *Sure,* and gets the binoculars. *I'll go sit*

on the dock and watch. We swim hard, float on our backs,
then swim some more. A breeze ripples the lake's surface.
Abi, like a swan in her white bathing suit, glides
through the water. I struggle beside her—nervous,

but also determined. We rest, swim on—and I make it
out to Anna's Island. We lie on the warm sand to dry,
then get ready to start back. I don't want to admit
how scared I am. What if— My worry is interrupted by

TJ in his little putt-putt motorboat. He waves,
circles back, slows down, and shouts, *Hey, you two!*

Abi says, *Hey,* and looks away. *Hi, TJ!* I yell.
He shuts off his motor and calls, *Where's your canoe?*

I answer, *We swam across.* I'm proud of that, but when
I think about swimming back . . . I'm not so sure.
Good for you, says TJ. *That's hard, even one way.*
You guys want a ride home? He puts his oars in the oar-

locks, rows in to catch our answer. Abi: *No thanks, we're good.*
Me: *Okay!* It's perfect that TJ showed up just in time to give me
a ride back. Abi looks away, combs her fingers through her hair.
TJ rests on his oars, holding his boat steady, waiting to see

if we'll agree. Abi finally says, *Okay.* TJ rows in and holds
out a hand to help us into the boat. Abi doesn't meet
his eyes—which I think is rude, but TJ doesn't seem
to notice. We sit together on the boat's middle seat.

You guys going to the fireworks tonight? he asks. *We were
planning to stay home, but that did not go down well with
the twins.* I can imagine. *We're not sure,* I say. *Everything
in our house these days revolves around what happens if*

the baby comes. He smiles. *When will that be?* he asks.
Any day, I say. *Have you picked a name?* he wonders. I say,
Maybe Pam and Dad have. I wouldn't know. I keep talking
to TJ, he keeps glancing at Abi, and Abi keeps looking away.

Fireworks

Claire

Some people like to drive into town for the big fireworks,
but we always go to the smaller event here at our little park.
Pam and Mrs. Johnson baked pies for the potluck, and we sit
with the Johnson family, waiting for it to get dark.

Sadie and Sophia catch fireflies in a jar, holding it close
to Devon's face so he can see their light. TJ doesn't like
being around so many people at once—that's why he never
goes to the beach. But he caught the biggest walleye pike

in a fishing contest, and he steps up to claim his trophy,
then brings it back to where we're sitting so we can all
admire it. *Where's Abigail?* asks Mr. Johnson. *She was here
a minute ago.* Dad looks around. Pam says, *She wants us to call*

her Abi now. I spot her, over there by her beach friends—
three girls, four boys. She's laughing and talking with Brock.
TJ is watching. I think I know how he feels—he might want to
go over there, but he's not sure how to join in that teenager talk.

Everyone who hasn't seen Dad since last summer congratulates
him and Pam on their marriage, and mentions the obvious baby.

Most of the year-round people, and some friends who
have summer cabins near ours, remember Mom. Maybe

they think it's good that Dad got married again—that
two daughters aren't enough family, and he needs a wife.
As I'm considering this, I overhear Ruth Gibson
say, *It's good to see Andrew getting on with his life.*

We're waiting for the fireworks to start when Abi comes back.
(Big smiles from TJ and the twins.) *Dad,* she says, *I want to go
into town for the fireworks. Okay?* At first, he thinks she means
we'd all have to leave, and she's asking him to drive us. *No,*

he says, *we're settled here. I like these fireworks.* She says,
*I don't mean the whole family. I mean, some kids I know are going,
and they asked me to go.* What kids? Whose parents are driving?
When would you get home? Oh, boy. What is Dad doing,

interrogating Abi like this, while her new friends (and TJ)
are listening to the whole thing? In the end, Dad won't let her
go, and they leave without her, so of course she's in a bad mood.
The twins snuggle up to her, and that seems to make her feel better.

Stormy Weather
Claire

Today is a rainy, stay-in-the-cabin, cozy kind of day.
Abi and Pam have a big jigsaw puzzle going.
Pam finds a piece of waterfall that fits, and Abi cheers
her on. Dad gives Abi his proud "you are growing

up" look—I'm not sure why. Maybe he likes how
Abi is including Pam. He gives my shoulder a squeeze
as I sit down at the table and then he flips a pancake
onto my plate. Outside the window, tall birch trees

bend and sway in the wind. *Looks like it's settling in
for a day or two,* says Dad. I used to like stormy weather
when Dad and Abigail and I would stay inside
and make popcorn and watch movies together.

But as the day goes on, nothing seems right. I keep
looking for the missing Mom-chair, or reaching
for one of her favorite books and remembering
it isn't here. Abi has a video that's teaching

her to draw people. She refuses to return the looks
I give her when Pam says something dumb,

such as: *I know! We could make ravioli out of leftover*
lasagna noodles. Abi? Claire? Who wants to come

and help spread peanut butter between two layers
of noodles and cut them into squares? She can't be
serious. I try to keep a straight face, but then
Dad asks, *Claire, why are you being so grouchy?*

Getting Closer
   Claire

It's been raining and windy for two days, and we're
feeling cooped up—too many people in this small
space. Pam is making a blanket for the baby,
and trying to teach Abi how to crochet, when all

of a sudden, out of nowhere, she announces,
They're getting closer. Is Abi as confused as I am?
Dad jumps up from the table—he seems to know
what Pam means. *I'll get the car,* he says, and Pam

starts grabbing things. What's going on? It's like
they've made a plan to leave us both behind
if aliens attack, and now the aliens are almost here—
or something. *Umm, Dad?* I say. *Would you mind*

explaining what's going on? I'm a little confused.
He looks at Abi and me and blinks. *Oh—*
he says, *Sorry, Claire. Pam meant—she's*
having contractions. We've talked about this. You know?

I stare at him. Okaaay—not aliens—it's the baby
who is almost here. Pam asks Dad, *Where*

did we put the suitcase I packed and brought from home?
He finds it in the front closet. *Abigail and Claire—*

he says, *Pam and I will be at the hospital tonight.*
I'll ask Mrs. Johnson to stop by, and I'll call you when the baby
comes. Abi looks up quickly and says, *You don't have to*
call the Johnsons! And, Dad, she adds, *remember? I'm Abi.*

The Johnson Family
Claire

An hour and a half after Dad and Pam drive off,
Mrs. Johnson calls and says Dad phoned her
when they got to the hospital. *Why don't you girls
come over here for supper,* she offers. I say, *Sure,*

what time? When I hang up, Abi glowers at me.
You could have asked me first. She changes her clothes.
And then changes them again. And again.
Tries to cover up a tiny pimple on her nose,

puts on two layers of lip gloss. *It's just the Johnsons,*
I remind her. *Come on—the rain has stopped. Let's go.*
The minute we walk in the door, Sadie and Sophia
jump all over Abi, and Devon wants to show

me some animals he made out of sticks and stones.
Whatever was annoying Abi seems to be okay.
But when TJ comes in and says, *Hi, Abigail,*
her face starts to get red, and she turns away

to start playing with the twins again. Is this about
the "Abi" thing? Does TJ remember that my sister

changed her name? I say, *She's calling herself Abi now.*
Sophia runs over and pulls me down to whisper,

TJ probably calls her his girlfriend. What?
No way. Did Abi hear her say that? If she did,
she's trying to ignore it. Mrs. Johnson says, *Claire,*
could you help Sadie set the table? She lifts a lid

from something that smells wonderful, and brings
it to the table just as Mr. Johnson brings in a plate
of hamburgers and veggies from the grill. TJ pours
lemonade in our glasses, and we sit down to eat.

I love this family. We talk about the baby coming,
and Sadie blurts out, *We're getting one too, next year.*
Mrs. Johnson shushes her, but smiles. *Yes,* she says,
your baby and ours can play together when you're up here.

I say, *You mean* their *baby. Pam and Dad's, not mine*
and Abi's. She starts to answer, but then Devon spills
his lemonade, and by the time TJ helps him clean up
the mess, the meal is almost over. Mrs. Johnson fills

a bag with food she thinks we'll like, and gives
it to us to take home. *We don't need it,* I say.
They'll be home tomorrow. And Abi says, *We're good.*
But Mrs. Johnson gives it to us anyway,

and says, *Call anytime if you need anything.* I mess up Devon's hair a little, hug the twins. TJ shoots a glance at Abi, but she's halfway down the path. He looks like he wanted to say good night, and missed his chance.

Shut Up About TJ
Claire

When we're walking home, I say,
You weren't very nice to TJ, and Abi snaps,
Just shut up about TJ! What? I haven't
said anything else about him. That's

the entire conversation. It makes me wonder
about what Sophia said. Does TJ want
Abi to be his girlfriend? That would be . . . different.
But since Abi is already acting mad, I don't

ask more questions. Right after we get home,
Dad calls to let us know there's no news
yet about the baby. *How long does this usually
take?* I ask, and he says, *No one ever knows,*

*sometimes just a few hours, but it can take a whole day
or even longer. Are you sure you're okay on your own?*
We assure him that we're fine. And we mean it.
At least I do. In a way, it's fun to be home alone.

Abi goes into our room and shuts the door.
I think she might be sleeping, so I open

the door carefully, just trying to be quiet, not
sneaking up on her or anything. But when I go in,

I see something that is either odd or pathetic
or—I decide this is it—very funny.
My sister is standing by the window
in the starlight, kissing Benjamin Bunny.

Speaking in the Dark
Claire

Abi knows I saw her. I manage not to laugh
by biting my cheeks and kind of blinking.
She's trying to pretend nothing unusual just
happened. I have no idea what she's thinking,

and I decide not to tease her, but I'm still
wondering about what Sophia said, because
it sort of makes sense. We go to bed, but we can't sleep.
Abi speaks into the dark, *Do you remember Mom?* I was

just a baby when lightning struck that day, so you'd
think my answer would be no. But sometimes the smell
of a coming storm cuts the air, like a knife so sharp
it draws blood before you know you touched it. I feel

thunder through the bottoms of my feet a heartbeat
before I hear it. *Maybe I do remember,* I tell Abi. *It's not
impossible. Babies have minds. They have eyes. Ears.
Don't you think I must have had a half-formed thought*

or two? Abi says, *Yes. I can't exactly hear her voice
anymore, but in my memory she rocks us, feeds*

us, dries our hair with a soft towel. I say, *Once she held me*
up to a frosty window, blew a hole with her warm breath. Seeds

in my imagination. Abi says, *When I'm swimming,*
and lie back on the waves, it's like something sings
to me and rocks me the way Mom did. Clouds in the shape
of her hair shift on the wind until they look like wings.

Our conversation opens a space, and Abi says, *Sorry*
I snapped at you on the way home. You know how
when you're worried about something, you might
get upset with the wrong person? Yes, I do, but wow,

I'm surprised to hear Abi admit that to me.
I ask, *What are you worried about?* And she says,
You know—boys. Kissing. Oh. *Umm . . . who are you*
planning to kiss? I ask. Brock would be my first guess,

but maybe TJ, or, who knows, maybe she's in love
with that stuffed rabbit. *I don't know,* she whispers.
And then she says, *Okay, I might as well tell you . . .*
I kissed TJ, corrects herself to say that TJ kissed her,

and adds, *It's hard to say. But anyway, you see why*
it's hard to talk to TJ now? I don't know what he's
thinking. Last year, it was just a practice kiss. But now
I think kissing should mean something. Don't you? She's

asking for advice, I think, but what do I know?
Before I say anything, she adds, *Also—what if I kiss*
someone and then find out I like someone else better?
She doesn't mention any names, but this

is not too hard for me to figure out: Abi likes Brock.
The only answer I come up with is: *Don't kiss anyone*
until you decide who you like best. That advice doesn't help.
But, Claire, she says (I hear her smile in the dark), *kissing is fun!*

Blake
Claire

We wake up early when the phone rings. It's Dad
calling to say, *Your baby brother is wide awake.*
He was born twenty minutes ago, and he is perfect—
just like his sisters. How do you like the name Blake?

I try to remember where I've heard it before.
Maybe in one of Mom's books? I tell Dad, *It's okay.*
Abi says, *I like it!* and Dad goes, *Well, good, that's settled.*
He makes it sound like we actually did have a say.

He tells us, *The baby and Pam are fine, but the doctor*
thinks it would be best if we stay here in town one more
night. Pam thinks I should drive back to check on things there.
I'm not sure—I told her you girls would be okay on your

own—what do you think? It's good to know he trusts us.
Don't come home, Abi says. *We'll be fine.* And I say, *Yup,*
we'll call if we need you, Dad. I can almost see Abi's thoughts
make a sharp turn onto kissing-street the minute we hang up.

Abi Swims Out to the Raft
Claire

Today is calm and sunny, and Dad's not home
to tell us what we should—or shouldn't—do.
We have lunch, then pack our backpacks
for the beach. Abi says, *Let's take the canoe.*

We paddle around Anna's Island, catching
the current, letting it carry us along. We plan
to avoid it on the way home. At the beach, Abi
walks up to the girls she met the other day. *Can*

I sit here? she asks. Brock and another boy are
on their way over. *Sure,* says one girl. *Meg, it's okay
if Abi sits here, right?* Meg smiles, nods—all the girls
treat Abi like a friend. I hope Jonilet comes today.

There she is, parking her bike. We find a place to sit
and watch the teenagers, listening to their laughter.
One after the other, they go in the water and dive
under the rope with a lot of splash and chatter.

As Abi swims out to the raft with them, her
voice carries across the water, a sweet clear

note in the chorus of girls' and boys' voices.
As I watch, one part of me wants to cheer

for Abi in the "Who Does Brock Like Best?"
contest. Another part says, "No, wait. I'm on TJ's
side." And still another part wants to go back
to a time when no one I knew cared about boys.

How Do You Know?
Conversation while canoeing home

Claire	Abi
	Did you see that, Claire?
What?	
	Meg, Trinity, and Shari Lee
	all like Brock—and he likes me!
How can you tell?	
	I'm the one he looked at first after he
	did a huge cannonball off the raft.
That's it?	
	That's the main one, but also
	he lifted the rope and held it up for me.
Oh.	
	And: he looked at me when
	he didn't think I was looking back.
How do you know?	
	Well . . . I was looking back.
So if he was looking at you,	
and saw you looking at him,	
will he think you like him?	
	Maybe. I don't know.
Let's change the subject.	
	Okay.
Are you excited about the baby?	

Claire	**Abi**
	Yes! Aren't you?
I guess so.	
It's going to be different, though.	
	Maybe in a good way.
Maybe.	
Abi, can you tie up the canoe by	
yourself?	
I think I'll take the kayak out	
for a little while.	

Not Ready
    Claire, in the kayak

Everyone knows **I**
    love my sister, but I **am**
        still a little sad. I'm **not**
            ready for this boy-talk, or **the**
                way that Abi, one of the **youngest**
            teenagers at the beach, fits right **in**
        with those girls—and boys. **Our**
    summers were always **family**
times. It's different **now**.

Telling the Neighbors the Baby Is Born
  The lake

Looks like Claire went
in the boathouse and found a life
vest her mom hung on a hook in there,
eleven years ago—it's still in good shape.

Now Claire seems peaceful, out here alone.
Or is she alone? Who's that, in his fishing boat,
there beside the fallen log, where herons wade?

Fred Gibson. He waves to Claire—she paddles
over and tells him the baby is born. *Ah,* he says.
Ruth has been wondering. I'll let her know. She'll

tell all our friends—you know how she is.
He chuckles. It's true—all along the
east shore, neighbor to neighbor,

everyone will hear about the
new baby before another
day goes by.

On the life vest Claire
found and pulled close around herself,

the faded name spelled *CARI*. She's made it
her own by adding an *L* and an *I*, and making an
E out of the final *I*: *CLAIRE*. I wonder where her

sister is this afternoon. Oh, I see her now—
over there, walking along the lake trail.
Not paying much attention, until she
glances up and sees TJ on the trail,

looking out over the water. *Hi, TJ. The baby
is born. He's coming home tomorrow. Dad says he's
very small and loud,* she says. TJ leans in to catch
every word, and Abi steps back a little bit.

I heard, says TJ. *Your dad called around
noon and told us. What do you*

think of the name Blake? He puts his
hands in his pockets, shifts his weight,
eager to see Abi, but both of them a little

awkward, now that they're alone.
Look! Abi says. *There's Claire,
out in the kayak. I better get back
now, before she comes home.
Guess I'll see you later.*

Abi Turns Away and TJ Stands There
Claire

I paddle away from Mr. Gibson in calm water—wait,
is that Abi, under the willow tree, by that big rock?
Is TJ with her? Maybe she's telling him she doesn't
want to kiss him, because now she likes Brock.

Abi turns away and TJ stands there looking at the lake.
I paddle in to shore, pull up the kayak, and tie it
to a tree, taking my time so I can wait for Abi. Here she
comes now, jogging down the lake trail. We're quiet

as we climb the steps up to the cabin. When we
get inside, I ask what she and TJ talked about.
I told him about the baby—that's all, she says.
He already knew. I came home when I saw you out

on the lake. The phone rings. Dad asks, *Everything okay?*
We say yes, and he says, *We'll be home tomorrow afternoon*
around five or so. Of course, Abi doesn't mention anything
about boys. *Bye, Dad,* she says. *Love you. See you soon!*

They Find a Place
Claire

It was so quiet in the cabin last night, we fell asleep
earlier than usual. This morning Abi went for a swim
before I woke up. Now she says, *Claire, they'll bring
Blake home this afternoon, and I want to be here to meet him.*

*Let's go to the beach before lunch, so we're sure to be back
when they get here.* We ride our bikes to the beach. Soon
Brock shows up and heads straight for Abi. Their friends
aren't here, and they find a place in the shade to sit, alone.

Pizza Pete's
Abi

Brock asks me if I want to go get lunch at Pizza Pete's.

    It's across the lake—less than an hour on our bikes—

        and there's no reason not to go. If we leave before everyone

else comes to the beach, I'll have a chance to get to know

    Brock on my own, and I'll be home before Dad and Pam

        come home with Blake. *Okay,* I say. *I'll let my sister know.*

I tell Claire, *We're going out for pizza.* She gives me a look—

    annoyed, suspicious? I don't know. *Will you quit it with*

        that "Dad won't like this" look? Oh, and we might stop by

Brock's house for a little while. Claire! How would Dad even know?

    I'll be back by two, and they won't be home till five. Is she mad

        because she wants to come, too? I'm sorry, but—no way.

Claire gets on her bike and pedals so fast she's out of sight

    before Brock and I leave. When we ride past our house,

        I see her bike on the grass, so I know she made it home okay.

Family
     Claire, in the kayak

Abi goes somewhere with a boy, and **I'm**

    not supposed to mind that we're **losing**

        this day we almost had together? **My**

            idea was: let's buy ourselves a **whole**

                chocolate-marble cake and a **family**-

                    size veggie pizza, and eat cake **first**

                without saving any for Pam and **Dad**.

            If Abi wants to take off with Brock—**and**

        ignore me completely—I guess it means **now**

    I can do whatever I want without telling **my**

plans to anyone, including my stupid **sister**.

Claire Paddles Around a Bend
The lake

Sun shines on these girls

here on the water. Claire: alone, maybe

enjoying this time when no one—not her

father and Pam, not Abi—knows where she is

or will worry if she paddles around the lake a

little farther. And Abi: standing on the end of a

dock—she's come with Brock to his house and

she holds out her phone to take a picture.

He stands beside her, smiling. She says,

Even if I can't post it, I can keep it to

remind me of this great day I've had

with you. She puts her phone back

in her pocket, and turns around, still smiling.

Nine ducklings swim by with their mother. Brock

gets closer to Abi. He speaks in a low voice,

slides an arm around her shoulder.

Abi looks happy, standing there
beside him. Perhaps they will kiss.
Or maybe not. Claire, in the kayak, glides
under a weeping willow that hangs out over
the water. She paddles hard, around a bend—

headed straight for her sister and Brock.
Early afternoon, the sun is shining
right in her eyes, blinding her

so she doesn't see Abi until it's too
late to retreat. She squints, sees their first
embrace. It looks a little bit uncomfortable—
each of them seems to be trying to figure out how to
position themselves for the kiss they must be quite sure
is about to happen. Then: Abi glances up and sees Claire.
No! she cries. Brock looks up. *What?* he says. Abi takes a
giant step to the side and tries to catch herself, but can't.

Claire stares at Abi for a split second, too far away to
help, as Abi waves her arms and falls off the dock
into my water. I'm sure Claire doesn't mean to
laugh, but she does. Abi comes up
dripping wet, gasping for air.

I Am Not
Claire

You're a snoop and a spy, Abi yells. I've never seen
her so mad. *It was a coincidence,* I keep insisting.
*Do you think I care enough to try to find out
where you and your stupid boyfriend are kissing?*

She yells again: *He's not stupid! Plus we didn't kiss.
AND he is not EVEN my boyfriend—thanks to you!
You better not tell Dad, you little creep.*
She tries to get me to take an actual vow:

I solemnly swear that I . . . So I tease her a little:
. . . am not a little creep. She balls up her hand
and for half a second I think she might
actually punch me. Then—*slam!*

She's out the door without saying where
she's going. Good—I hope she stays gone.
Maybe she'll get lost in the woods or something,
and cool off a little. I like being home alone.

It Won't Ever Be
Abi

I'm going for a long walk, where I won't see

      anyone I know. The opposite way down the trail

            from TJ's house, because what would I say if I saw him?

And nowhere near the beach, where Brock

      is probably telling everyone how my little sister

            spied on us and laughed when I fell off his dock.

Away from Claire for an hour or so. She wants

      everything to be exactly the same as it's always been.

            Well, guess what? It's not, and it won't ever be again.

A Spy and a Snoop
Claire

Abi's been gone for half an hour. If she's
out somewhere with a boy, I don't care.
She can do whatever she wants.
What I want to know is, where

are Mom's things? If Pam got rid of them,
what would she do with them? Where are they
now? With everyone gone, this might be
a good chance to find out. Okay . . .

I go in and look under Dad and Pam's bed.
Nothing but dust. (. . . *you little creep*)
I open their closet. Start with Pam's side.
So many clothes. (. . . *a snoop and a spy*) I keep

looking: Yoga mat. Organized shoe shelves.
("Stack summer shoes in rainbow order;
make it easy to match any outfit"—Abi and I
laughed together about that "Pointer

from Pam" just last month.) Pam is so boring—
none of this is what I'm looking for.

What are you . . . (Who's that?
I didn't hear anyone open the door.)

. . . *doing in their closet?* Abi! I scramble out.
Now who's spying? Oh—I left the door ajar,
that's why I didn't hear her come in. *I know,*
she says. *You're proving my point. You really are*

a snoop and a spy. A little creep. Arms crossed over
her chest, she looks down at me. *If,* she says,
you put everything back, just like you found it,
I solemnly swear—pause for effect, she raises

a hand—*I won't tell Dad . . . or Pam.* So: we're even.
We each have our own little secret we don't
want the other to tell—almost as good as trust.
Abi stares at me until I agree. *Okay. I won't*

tell Dad you want to kiss a boy you barely know, just
because the other girls think he's cute, and who knows where
Brock's parents were when you were there, so I think—
Abi interrupts. *I don't care what you think, Claire.*

Don't Talk About Your Mother
Claire

Abi . . . I say. We're on the porch, waiting for Dad and Pam
to get home. I think she's calmed down. *Are you still mad?*
A heartbeat or two. *I guess not,* she says. Good, because
something's on my mind. *Have you noticed*, I ask, *how Dad*

never talks about Mom anymore? Abi says, *Yeah, I know.*
She sighs and says, *It's almost like he made a new rule:
Don't talk about your mother in front of my wife.* I'm glad
she understands. *Sometimes,* I say, *I miss Dad, that's all.*

Now We Are Five
  Claire

Dad's car is coming up the road, it's turning in,
it's here. He and Pam get out, open the back door,
and Dad lifts out a tiny baby wrapped in a soft
blanket. Our family of three became four

last year, and now when they come inside, we are five.
Abigail, Dad says (she doesn't correct him), *Claire, meet
your brother, Blake.* He pulls back the blanket. *Oh, Dad!*
I'm surprised to hear myself say. *He's so tiny. So sweet.*

Try Holding Him
Claire

Even Blake, small as he is, loves Abi. When Dad
and Pam brought him home yesterday, Abi
learned right away how to wrap a soft blanket
around him and rock him like he's her own baby.

Now I watch her and Pam and Dad hold him—
they all know exactly how to do it so he doesn't cry.
But when I sit down and Pam puts him in my arms,
he screws up his face and squawks and squirms. *Try*

holding him on your other side, Abi suggests. I bump
his head as I'm switching arms, and he lets out a scream.
I didn't mean to hurt him, I say. Pam takes him back,
and asks Dad to bring her some special cream

to put on the bump. He gets her huge purple bag
of baby supplies and dumps things out on the floor
to find it. I try saying, *Sorry,* but no one hears.
Blake is still crying when I slip out the back door.

Quiet

      Claire, in the kayak

Early evening is **when**

      I try to make **everything**

            seem right. The cabin **is noisy**

                  with Blake drowning out **the quiet**,

                      so I come out on the lake at **sunset**

                  and watch birds float **on the water**

            as if weightless. This hour **gives me**

      time to think and breathe, **a sliver**

of sunset, a moment **of calm**.

Tyger Tyger
     Claire

Dad's voice is strong and gentle:
Tyger Tyger, burning bright . . .
as he lays his little black-haired baby
down to sleep . . . *in the forest of the night.*

Probably. Yes. Of Course.

Claire	*Abi*
Do you think Dad loved us like that when we were babies?	
	Probably. Yes. Of course he did.
And Mom?	
	Her, too.
You know that poem Dad's been saying?	
	"Tyger Tyger, burning bright"?
Yes, that one. Dad says it's "Tyger," spelled with a y.	
	I know, I saw it in one of Mom's books.
They should call the baby Tyger.	
	You mean we?
He's their baby. I don't think we get a say.	

He's Avoiding Me
Claire

Blake sleeps a lot, but when he's awake, he's the king
of the house. Which suits Abi just fine—Dad's so busy
with the baby, or asleep during the day because he's been
up all night, that his usual eagle eye on us is a little fuzzy.

It's been two days since they came home. That was the day
Abi fell off the dock, and now when we're in our room alone,
she worries, *I must have looked ridiculous.* She has a jar of rice
in the closet because she heard you can dry out a phone

by putting it in rice, to absorb the water. (It hasn't worked.)
She tells Dad, *We're going to the beach.* He says, *Have fun.*
Brock doesn't come at first, and Abi says, *He's avoiding me.*
She sits with Jonilet and me, telling Jonilet, *I felt so dumb*

when I fell in the water. She's sure Brock doesn't like
her now, but I'd be surprised. If anything, I'd guess
I'm the one he doesn't like. *Who cares anyway?* I ask,
and Abi glares at me. *Let's go swimming,* Jonilet suggests.

While Jonilet and I are doing handstands near the rope,
Abi swims out to the raft by herself. I don't recognize

the boy she starts talking to, and can't hear what they say.
Jonilet comes up for air, wipes water from her eyes,

and tells me, *That's Brock's friend Josh. He has a lot of parties.*
Then Abi swims in, happy. *I got invited to a bonfire! Let's go
home,* she says. Wait—Abi just met this boy. Did he
ask her out? She has to realize Dad will say no.

He Didn't Say No
Claire

Supper: Abi, Dad, and me at the kitchen table.
Pam changing Blake in the other room. *Did you*
have any adventures today? Dad asks. *My bike chain*
came off, I tell him. Abi hesitates, then says: *I got invited to—*

Pam calls, *Honey, could you bring me the baby wipes?*
Dad gets up to find them. Abi whispers, . . . *a bonfire.*
I said I'd go, okay? She smiles at me. *He didn't say*
no, she observes, nodding at Dad's empty chair.

Cover for Me
Claire

Why don't you just tell Dad where you're going?
I ask. Abi curls her hair and traces pink
around her lips. *Because,* she explains, *he'd say
no—duh! You know how way-too-strict he is. I think*

Brock will be there, and, according to Josh,
he still likes me. Brushing on mascara.
Wait—are you going with Josh? I ask. Abi rolls
her eyes. *No,* she says. Blinking at the mirror.

It's at his house. I'm walking—by myself.
It's only a couple of miles, she says. *Claire, please—*
cover for me if you have to. She squirts an orangey
smell in her hair that stays in our room after she's

closed the door. She goes to check the kitchen.
The coast is clear: Dad's sitting with Pam and Blake
on the front porch, and Abi slips out the back door,
leaving me to pretend she's in our room—it's so fake.

A Drumbeat
   Abi

I've walked two miles around the east end of the lake.
      It wasn't hard to find Josh's house, but now I'm here,
            it's getting dark, and I'm not sure I should have come.

The bonfire burns high and bright. Music. Laughter.
      Do I know anyone? Should I turn around and leave
            before I'm seen, go home before the night gets darker?

A drumbeat. Silhouettes of people dancing.
      Someone playing music. I step in a little closer.
            Faces in the firelight—it's Brock, on the guitar.

On each side of him, a girl is singing. (Trinity on one side,
      Shari Lee on the other.) I know that song. Meg is dancing
            with two friends. I stand at the edge of the circle of light,

deciding: Turn and go home? Or stay to see what happens?
      Brock looks up, sees me, and doesn't look away. Trinity
            and Shari Lee smile and say, *Hi, Abi.* I decide to stay.

Where's Abi?
Claire

How long will it take Dad to notice
that one of his daughters isn't home?
Pam puts Blake in his cradle, and when he cries
Dad picks him up and walks around the room

a million times. He puts the baby on his shoulder,
bounces him, pats him, sings to him, and rocks
him. Blake looks up with his big baby eyes
wide open, looks at me when Dad walks

past—was that a smile? I try smiling back. *He's pooping,*
Pam explains as she takes him from Dad, sings more
baby songs, changes him and puts him down again.
It's been three hours since Abi slipped out the back door,

without really telling Dad where she was going,
how she was getting there, when she would be
home. When Blake finally goes to sleep, Pam asks,
Where's Abi? and Dad goes, *Who? Oh, you mean*

Abigail. Have you seen her, Claire? I hate this. *Umm . . .*
not for a while, I say. Dad looks puzzled, so I add,

Maybe she's in our room with headphones on. Is that a lie?
Not exactly; he can check if he wants to. But Dad

says, *Blake kept us awake a lot last night. We're turning in.*
He locks the doors, switches off the porch light,
yawns, and turns away. I'll unlock the back door later.
Good night, Dad, I say. He and Pam reply, *Good night.*

White T-Shirt
Abi

In the circle of light around the fire, a dancer falls
      and sprains her ankle. She's crying, and she's
            trying to stand up, but falls again. The music

and the dancing stop. What happened? One minute
      she's dancing, the next she's on the ground, and can't
            stand up. *What's your name?* I ask. *Regina,* she answers

through her tears. *She stepped in a rabbit hole,* says Josh.
      Her ankle starts to swell. I took first aid last year, and I
            know what to do. There's a cooler of ice right over there.

Brock brings it to me. I sit down beside Regina so she
      can rest her ankle on my knee. *What can we put ice in?*
            I ask Brock. He takes off his white T-shirt and ties it shut

to make an ice pack, which I put on Regina's ankle.
      She stops crying, and Josh brings his older sister,
            Annie, who asks Regina, *Can you walk to my car?*

She isn't sure. Brock and Annie help her stand
      and try to walk. She stumbles, so they make a chair
            out of their arms and carry her. She gets in the backseat,

and I get in beside her to hold the ice against her ankle.

Annie says, *I know where Regina lives. It's not far.* She
starts the car. Brock opens the door and squeezes in

beside me. *I'll help you hold the ice,* he says. Regina
stretches out her leg across our knees. *Abi, it's a good
thing you knew what to do,* Brock says. He doesn't seem

to be thinking about me falling off his dock. *It's nice of you,*
I say, *to literally give her the shirt off your back.* Brock smiles.
Abi, I like you more and more. Not everyone can use the word

"literally" correctly. (I never knew vocabulary
could impress a boy.) It's a little crowded here
in the backseat of this car. Brock lifts his arm

behind me, drops his hand to let it rest lightly
on my shoulder. So—Brock without his shirt.
A mix of bonfire smoke and boy-smell in the car.

And those words: *I like you more and more.* Annie
is driving slowly along the bumpy road, but we
can't help leaning into each other around every curve.

After we take Regina home, Annie asks, *Abi, should I drop
you off now?* Brock shakes his head a tiny bit. *No,* I say.
Thanks, but I'll go back to the bonfire and walk home later.

Now Under the Stars
The lake

Lapping at the shore,
I'm enjoying this party, reflecting both
firelight and the light of a half-moon. Someone stirs the
embers and feeds the fire with pine. Abi left some time ago

in a car with several others. When she returns, the girl who
sprained her ankle isn't with her, but Brock is at her side.

Walking toward the fire, he reaches out to take her
hand. She turns to him with an easy smile,
as if she does this all the time. He smiles,
too. They stand beside the fire talking.

It seems they've forgotten all about
the disaster of Abi falling

in the water. They walk toward me,
stand together on the shore, quiet. Then

Abi kicks off her shoes and steps into my water.
Brock does the same. At first, they're looking
out at me, then at each other, and now
under the stars—no interruption
this time—they kiss.

Footsteps on the Gravel Path
Claire

After midnight. Moonlight shining through
my window, leaf-shadows on the wall
dancing above Abi's empty bed. I'm listening
hard, and waiting—finally, I hear footsteps fall

lightly on the gravel path. *Claire,* Abi whispers
at our window, *is Dad still up?* Her face is flushed,
her eyes are shining. *I'll check,* I whisper back, then,
No. So she comes in the back door. After she's brushed

out the tangles in her hair, she climbs into bed, still
smiling. I turn off the light, but she is wide awake.
Brock likes me, Claire, and I like him, she says.
Loons call back and forth, out on the lake.

Some Kind of Makeup
Claire

Abi wakes up later than usual, decides
to skip her early-morning swim. She puts on
her favorite running clothes and some
kind of makeup that, after she's done

designing her face, is supposed to look like
she's not wearing it, except for a thin black
line she carefully draws on each eyelid.
I'm going running, she tells me. *I'll be back*

before Dad has finished breakfast. Which she is not.
When she comes in two hours later, Pam and Dad
don't ask any questions. Up at three with Blake, they
didn't get much sleep, and they're still bleary-eyed.

Two Boys
Abi

Brock and I agreed we'd meet this morning

      and go running together. It's not a secret,

            but I don't mention it to Dad and Pam.

After Brock leaves, I walk down to the lake,

      and I see TJ in his boat. He rows over to our dock,

            all smiles. I remember how easy our friendship

used to be—maybe it could still be like that. I say, *Hi, TJ.*

      He says, *Hi, Abi.* I say, *It's a beautiful day.* (Good start.)

            He asks, *Want to go for a walk?* And I think: *I'd enjoy that.*

Maybe I'd find a way to tell him I like Brock. But I say,

      No thanks. I don't give him a reason. I never expected

            two boys to like me at once, and I'm not sure what to do.

Squirrels Chasing Each Other
Claire

Pam puts Blake in my arms, and a miracle
happens: he doesn't scream. I have to admit
I'm starting to get used to him—he might even
like me a little bit. He's just had a bath, and I sit

near the window holding him, all wrapped
up in a towel with yellow ducks on it—I'm
okay with this. I breathe in the smell of his
clean baby hair, and watch a gray squirrel climb

up a tree outside the window—then two
squirrels, chasing each other around the tree,
and down the path toward the lake. Who is that
on the dock? Abi. And—I think it's Brock. He

must have stayed here after they went running.
I crane my neck, but the trees block my view.
Blake is happy—I don't want to get up
to walk over to a different window.

When Pam takes Blake from my arms, I look out
at the place I think I saw Abi and Brock,

but now I don't see Brock down there.
Wait—is that TJ's boat, tied to our dock?

I don't see him anywhere. Would he hide and
spy on Brock and Abi? *I'm going out in the kayak,*
I tell Dad. Once I'm out on the lake, I can just—
not being nosy or anything—look back.

From Out Here
   Claire, in the kayak

From out here on the lake, not too far from shore, **it**
      looks like TJ is rowing home in his boat. He **makes**
            a better spy than I do, looking back as if to make sure **no**
      one's watching. There's Abi now. If he had any **sense**,
he'd stay out of sight. But he waves—to Abi, not **to me**.

Abi Doesn't Want to Talk
Claire

I'm not sure what's going on with Abi. Two days
have gone by with no real conversation. I think she's
avoiding me: going to bed each night before I do,
and getting up while I'm still sleeping. These

days, with a baby in the house, everyone's too busy
to do the things we usually do together.
Is there something Abi doesn't want to talk about?
She isn't talking much to Dad and Pam either.

Grounded
Claire

This is not good—Dad comes in from his first time
out fishing since Blake was born. *Abigail?* In that
one word I hear a mountain of trouble. Abi must
hear it, too, but she tries not to show it. *What?*

(Innocent as Blake when he yawns and stretches.)
Were you at a bonfire party Sunday night? A direct
question, not even "Where were you on Sunday?"
She's trapped. *What do you mean?* She tries to deflect

Dad's question, which doesn't work. *I mean,* he says,
*were you at a bonfire party Sunday night? I heard about
it from Fred Gibson when I was out fishing. He told me
his granddaughter sprained her ankle, and you went out*

of your way to help her get home—at ten o'clock at night?
Abi tries again: *This girl, Regina, got hurt and we put ice
on her ankle, and Josh's sister, Annie, drove her home
and I went along to help. I was trying to be nice.*

Dad is not so easily distracted. It takes him about five
minutes to get all the details out of her—well, most

of them—ten seconds more to ground her
for a week. *No fair!* she argues. *Dad! At least*

let me go to the beach—with Claire, she adds, like I'd
be her chaperone. *No, Abigail,* Dad starts to insist.
But Abi gets him to agree: *You can go to the beach.*
Nowhere else—and only with Claire. Abi can't resist

a thumbs-up to me, behind Dad's back. When he leaves
the room, she says, *You're on my side, right? Who even does*
that? Dad should know grounding kids doesn't work. He can be
so old-fashioned. Oh boy. I can't wait to see how this goes.

Claire, Let's
Claire

So now I am my big sister's babysitter: *Claire, let's go*
out in the canoe. Claire, let's ride our bikes to the beach.
Dad, can Claire and I get up early and go swimming?
Only, once we're out of sight, out of Dad's reach,

especially anywhere in the vicinity of Brock,
she's like, *You can go now.* After three days of this,
I'm about ready to disown her. Dad can hire
a professional security guard to keep tabs on his

beautiful, sneaky daughter. How am I supposed to
do it? Now we're at the beach, and I don't know where
Abi is. Jonilet comes up to me and says, *I saw your sister*
in the woods with Brock. Want to see if they're still there?

I don't know about this, but here goes. We walk slowly
down the trail and—there they are, leaning against a tree,
kissing! We turn around before they see us, and after
a while Abi comes back and tries to convince me

she'd just gone off on her own for a little stroll.
That is annoying enough, but then on the way home

we see TJ and he asks Abi if she wants to go out
for a boat ride after dinner. *Sorry,* she says, *I'm*

grounded—maybe Dad would let me if Claire comes along.
Which obviously is *not* what TJ has in mind. It's clear,
even to me, that he likes Abi the way she likes Brock.
(I don't remember TJ being like this last year.)

Dad Didn't Say
Claire

Dad wants to take Pam out for dessert to celebrate
her birthday tonight. *If we get Blake to sleep,*
could you girls babysit for an hour or so? he asks.
I'm surprised—Blake is barely a week

old—but it's good they trust us. *Okay,*
I say. I look at Abi, and she seems to be less
sure, maybe worried about what we'll do if Blake
wakes up crying. She thinks for a minute, then, *Yes,*

she says, *we can do that.* As soon as Dad's not looking,
she slips out with the landline and comes back
smiling. After dinner, Pam gives Blake a bath,
sings him to sleep, and changes into a short black

dress, with black-and-gold sandals. She and Dad
go out the front door. Ten minutes later: a knock
on the back door. *Dad didn't say no one could come over,*
says Abi with a little smile. Surprise, surprise: it's Brock.

He comes in for about two minutes; then they go
out on the porch while I stay inside in case Blake

wakes up. I hear them talking and laughing together
as the sun splashes red and orange on the lake.

Blake stays asleep. Abi and Brock come in when the sky
turns dark, with a splash of stars and an almost-full moon.
Brock barely talks to me. He leaves when Abi says,
Dad and Pam will be getting home pretty soon.

Don't Tell Dad
Claire

Abi does this big showy yawn, stretches, and says,
I've had a long day. I think I'll go to bed early tonight.
She hugs Dad, then Pam. (She's been doing that
ever since their shopping spree.) In a too-bright

voice, she adds, *Happy birthday, Pam! Good night!*
Blake is awake and Pam asks, *Want to hold him, Claire?*
I say, *Sure.* I'm getting to like him more and more,
his wrinkly little nose, these soft curls in his hair.

Dad, Pam, Blake, and I stay up another hour after Abi
puts on her "good night" show. At ten-fifteen, I give
Blake back to Pam, hug Dad, and head to bed.
What? Seriously? Does my sister think I can live

in the same room with her for my entire life, and be
tricked into thinking two or three pillows under
her blanket are actually her, fast asleep? Where is she?
The screen is pushed up about an inch. I wonder . . .

I bet she climbed out the window to go meet Brock.
Don't tell Dad. She doesn't even have to say it,

or leave a note; she just assumes I'll do what she
wants—that I'll know I have to stay awake and wait.

When we were small, Dad would come in every night
to tell us stories and sing to us before we went to sleep.
Around the time he married Pam, I guess he thought we
were too old for that, but sometimes he still tries to keep

up the old tradition. What if he comes in tonight
and notices that Abi isn't here *and* she's trying
to pull off this pillows-and-blanket trick?
He'd ask me where my sister is—and I stink at lying.

A Path of Moonlight
Abi

Let's meet at the dock, and go for a night swim.
      We made our plan when Brock came over.
            At first he said, *I don't have my swim trunks.*

But I convinced him to go home and put them on
      under his clothes. *Come back at ten o'clock,* I said.
            I threw a towel over my shoulders, climbed out

my window into the night, and now we're swimming,
      quiet as we can—kicking underwater, gliding along
            a path of moonlight toward Anna's Island. *Look,* I whisper:

An owl soars to the top of a tree whose branches
      sweep clouds from the sky: a sudden, long-ago
            memory of Mom brushing hair out of my eyes.

Night Swimmers
   The lake

What are they doing? I
hold these crazy youngsters
as they swim out into the night
toward the island. My strong

current will help them
at first, on the way there, but
not on the way back. Of course

Abi knows about that, but Brock is
not as good a swimmer as she thinks he is.
Yes, he said when Abi asked if he could swim
out to the island and back. He plunged right in.
Now they're out where the water gets deeper.
Either he will find out he can do it, or this is

going to be harder than they thought.
I'm impressed, so far. He's trying
very hard. But will he become
exhausted before Abi does?

You're sure your sister won't tell
on you? he asks. Abi answers, *Yes, I'm sure.*
Unless . . . If she got scared, then I think she might.

Good—they're floating on their backs now,
resting for a while, looking at the sky,
enjoying the full moon, the stars,
and their own quiet conversation on
this warm midsummer night. Still full of
energy, neither of them seems anxious to
return. *Abi, look—two loons, swimming right*

toward us, whispers Brock. *Where?* Abi asks.
He stretches out his arm and lightly touches
Abi's shoulder as he points out the loons.
Now, Brock and Abi swim on together.

No one in the world knows they're
out here. This is dangerous.
Which means: exciting.

I Need Your Help
Claire

It's almost midnight when Abi shows up at our window.
Claire! she whispers. *Is Dad up?* This time, I refuse to check
for her. *How should I know?* I ask. I keep my voice down,
but that's as much as I'll do to help. If she wants to trick

Dad, she can do it on her own. She pushes up the screen,
climbs in, and perches on the edge of her bed. She's
wearing her swimsuit, and her hair is wet—it's obvious
she's been night-swimming! *Claire,* she whispers, *please,*

Brock and I need your help. Get dressed! Shhh . . . I'll explain
when we get outside. She puts on dry clothes, grabs a towel
and a dark green hoodie, and climbs back out the window.
I don't know what to think—I get dressed and follow.

As we walk down to the lake, Abi tells me she and Brock
swam to Anna's Island in the moonlight. Halfway
back, Brock got too tired to keep swimming, so now
he's waiting for her on the sandbar. *It's chilly,* I say.

I know, Abi says. *Brock was shivering when I left him—*
that's why I need your help. We'll get there faster if the two

of us paddle as hard as we can. We put the canoe in the water,
I get in the front, Abi pushes us off, and we head into

the moonlight. It's so peaceful I almost forget how mad I am.
At the sandbar, Brock is doing jumping jacks to keep warm.
Abi gives him the towel and the hoodie. *Why didn't you bring
my clothes?* he asks. *Oh!* says Abi. *I forgot.* He puts his arm

around her. *It's okay. Thanks,* he says. She gives him a kiss,
and says, *We should thank Claire. She really helped us out.*
I'm sure, to Brock I'm only Abi's pesky little sister,
but he does say, *Thanks, Claire. I've heard about*

*the current in this part of the lake—but it's stronger than I thought.
Could you drop me off at my house, so I won't have to walk home
from your dock?* Abi hesitates. *Okay, I guess so,* she says, then
whispers to me, *Let's hope Dad doesn't get up and go in our room.*

We Paddle Past the Island
Claire, in the canoe

Brock and Abi paddle while **I**

    sit in the canoe, watching. I **want**

        to be as strong as Abi—I try **to**

            keep up, but she can run, **swim**,

                paddle—all better than me. We get **to**

                    Brock's and he gets out, wearing **the**

                green hoodie. We paddle past the **island**,

        so beautiful, bathed in moonlight—**and**

      head home. *Oh!* Abi says. *A light in the **back***

  room. I don't answer. I'm on the lake **with-**

out permission—in as much trouble as **Abi**.

An Owl Hoots
Claire

We tie up the canoe as silently as we can, and
tiptoe up the path to the cabin. Blake is crying,
so we wait in the dark until he stops, then
sneak around to our window, trying

not to step on a branch or make any
kind of sound. We hear a coyote howl,
and Dad steps onto the porch to look around.
I don't think he sees it, or us. An owl

hoots from the top of a tall pine. It's scary
in a good way, outside at night. We keep an eye
on our window after Dad goes in, hoping
he doesn't open the door to our room. I

don't even dare whisper to Abi. Finally,
all the lights in the cabin are out—Dad must
be back in bed. We stay outside for about
half an hour longer, until we can trust

that everyone is asleep. Then we push up
the screen and climb in. I've never been so glad

to bury my face in my pillow. Abi picks up
Benjamin Bunny and whispers, *We're back.*

Think, Claire, Think
Claire

Did I have a wild dream, I ask, *or did that really happen
last night?* I can tell by the sun, we've woken up late.
Abi blinks a few times before answering. *It happened
all right. Lucky we didn't get*— She stops. *Oh, no. Wait . . .*

She jumps up and pulls on the first clothes she finds,
runs into the kitchen and out the back door. I look
through the window and see her tearing down the path
to the dock. When I go in the kitchen, Pam says, *Abi took*

off running like her life depended on it. What's up?
Blake peeks over Pam's shoulder. She pats him
on the back, and he looks around like he, too, wants
to know what's going on. *Maybe she's going for a swim*

before breakfast? I really have no idea. While I'm eating
my cereal, Abi comes running back in, all out of breath.
Where's Dad? she asks, and Pam says, *He got up to go fishing
this morning around five o'clock. Is anything wrong? I expect*

him back soon. Abi says, *No, nothing's wrong. Claire,*
she adds, *I'm going back down to the dock—come with me?*

I just remembered—I have to keep you with me at all times.
I don't mind going with her, but why the urgency?

As soon as we get outside, she tells me: *They're not there!*
(What's not where?) *Brock's clothes and shoes were on our dock*
when we went swimming. I forgot to pick them up when we
got back last night. If Dad went fishing at five o'clock,

he must have found them. I am SO busted. You have to help
me come up with an explanation. Think, Claire, think.
Let's see . . . *Some stranger,* I suggest, *wandered by, dove into*
the water, and drowned—he must have had too much to drink,

we better call 911? That might distract everyone for a while.
Except they'd drag the lake for a body, which they wouldn't find.
Seriously, Abi—you got yourself into this, don't expect me
to get you out. Suddenly her face lights up, her brilliant mind

at work again. *Maybe,* she says, *Brock remembered in time.*
He got up early to go running, and came and got his clothes
before Dad went fishing. She's desperate enough to believe it.
Right, Abi, I say. *Why were you even worried? Who knows,*

maybe he swam over here, just to prove he could do it.
We hear a boat—Dad? Abi gets a panicky look on her face.
Maybe he won't ask any questions, she says. Then the boat
comes closer and we see: It's not Dad's boat. It's TJ's.

Thanks, TJ
Claire

TJ pulls up to our dock, shuts off his motor, and says,
Strangest thing—I got up at four-thirty to go fishing, and I
swung by your place to see if your dad might be going out—
had some extra bait I thought he might use. I wondered why

these clothes were on the end of your dock. Seemed like
someone must've gone in swimming—but no one was in the water.
Abi keeps her face still. *Looked like rain,* TJ adds, *so I picked them up*
and put them in this bag. Like a lamb that was headed to slaughter

and escaped on the way, Abi smiles and accepts TJ's gift.
He ties up his boat, gets out. *Hey,* he says, *you guys want the fish*
I caught this morning? I take the fish, and Abi says, *Thanks, TJ!*
She grabs him and gives him a big hug—and a little kiss.

A Friend-Kiss
Abi

Claire, would you just shut up about who I'm kissing?

    I don't even know what you mean about TJ! He knows

        we're just friends. Believe me, boys can tell the difference

between a friend-kiss and the other kind. TJ is almost like

    a brother to me. He's nice to me because he's a nice person,

        that's all. I don't know if he knew whose clothes those were,

or how they happened to be on our dock. I don't have to

    explain it to him. Or to you. If I want to give him a TINY little

        thank-you kiss on his cheek, how exactly is that hurting you?

Rivals
Claire

How did I get in the middle of this? TJ sees me out
on our dock, dangling my feet in the water. He rows
over and says, *Hey, Claire, can I ask you something?*
I nod, and he says, *Do you know how those clothes*

got on your dock last night? I don't care what Abi says;
I know TJ wants to be her boyfriend, and I bet he thinks
he could be. He has a right to know. *A boy,* I answer,
left them there when he went in swimming. TJ blinks

a few times as he puts the story together in his mind.
Would this boy be named Brock? He laughs out loud
when I don't answer. *So when I thought I was helping
Abi,* he says, *I was helping my rival even more. Proud*

to be of assistance, sir, he jokes. His rival! I knew it.
At least he thinks it's funny, and I bet I can make
him laugh even more. I tell him the whole story, and he
does laugh—but then he gets serious. *This lake,*

he says, *has a strong current that goes around the
island. I see that guy, Brock, out running all the time,*

but I don't see him much out on the lake, or swimming
long distance like Abi does. No surprise he couldn't do it—I'm

just surprised Abi didn't tell him it's a lot harder
than you think it will be. Tell her to be careful. As if
I could. *She doesn't listen to warnings like that,* I say,
especially not from me. TJ holds his boat still with

his oars and says, *Thanks for letting me know, Claire.*
(I'm not sure I should have, but he's welcome.) *How's it*
going? he asks. *For you, I mean.* I splash my foot in the water
and think about that. *Okay, I guess. The baby can get a little bit*

annoying. He's cute and everything, but sometimes that's all
Dad and Pam can think about. TJ gives me a friendly smile.
I know, he says, and adds, *I could row out to the island with you*
sometime, so you can try swimming back—that's a tough half-mile.

It Means a Lot
Claire

Is Dad trying to make us feel guilty, or is he doing it
without trying? *Thanks for babysitting last night, girls,*
he says. *It means a lot to have daughters I can trust.*
I don't look at Abi. I stir my soup, making little swirls

of noodles as Dad goes on. *Since Pam and I went out*
for dessert last night, why don't the three of us go
somewhere tomorrow—maybe over to Pizza Pete's?
I say, *Okay!* And Abi says, *Sure, Dad.* Does Dad know

how much we miss doing things with him? This
makes me happy—it shows Dad really does care
about Abi and me as much as he cares about Blake. Plus,
for once, I won't be Abi's babysitter—Dad will be there.

A Quick Turn
Claire

I'm going into town this afternoon, but I'll be back by four
at the latest, to take my two special girls on our big date.
Dad can be so corny. *So,* he says, *if you go to the beach,*
make sure you're home by then. I don't want to be late

for our exclusive reservation at Pizza Pete's. I requested
the best table, and the maître d' will be waiting for us.
Pam smiles; on her birthday, they did go to a
fancy restaurant like that—Pizza Pete's is just

the opposite. *Check the weather,* Dad says. *There could*
be storms coming through later on. Abi says, *Okay,*
but once Dad's gone, she's more interested in how
to get Brock's clothes back to him sometime today.

She thinks he'll be at the beach, and she puts his clothes
in her backpack before we set off in the canoe. It's hotter
than it's been all summer, so we're sticking close
to shore, where weeping willows hang over the water.

We're coming to the place where I went around the bend
and surprised Abi and Brock that day she fell off his dock.

133

I start to paddle harder, in a hurry to get past his house,
but then I hear Abi's startled whisper: *Is that Brock?*

She lifts her paddle to point at him. He's not looking
our way, but Abi is staring at a girl, who is. She sits
on the end of his dock, and Brock is putting sunscreen
on her shoulders. Abi squints, trying to see them, but it's

bright; the sun is in her eyes. She twists her paddle
to make a quick turn. The girl gives a little wave,
which Abi does not see, as we paddle back the way
we came. I turn to face Abi and say, *Don't we have*

to take Brock's clothes back to him? She looks like she's
about to cry. *Why would he have another girlfriend*
so soon after he told me he liked me? It doesn't even make
sense. True, I guess—so does this mean the end

of her sneaking out and lying and deceiving Dad,
which I am completely sick of? I can't resist
saying out loud: *I wonder if this is how TJ feels.*
(Was that mean?) *That's different!* Abi tries to insist,

but that's all she says. Maybe she's actually thinking
about it—she's quiet the rest of the way home.
Thunder rumbles in the distance as we pull up the canoe
and tie it to the tree. Abi mutters, *I just feel so dumb.*

Glad We Can Talk
Claire

Dad gets back from town and helps Pam
feed Blake and put him to bed. *Okay, who*
is ready for our big evening out? he asks. *Abi, is*
anything wrong? She shrugs, and he says, *You*

seem quiet. I just wondered. We drive to Pizza Pete's,
sit in a booth by the window, and the waiter
brings us our drinks. Dad proposes a toast:
To my girls—who are growing up too fast. We lift our

plastic cups. *Don't worry, Dad. We're still kids,* I say.
Speak for yourself. I'm not a kid, Abi has to add.
Either way, says Dad, *as I've said before, it means*
a lot to be able to trust you two right now. Abi, I'm glad

your week of being grounded is almost over. I hope
it hasn't been too hard on you, and that you've learned
a little bit. He takes a big bite out of his pizza, and
doesn't seem to notice that Abi's face has turned

bright red. She looks out the window, away
from Dad. He and I each eat two whole pieces

before Abi takes a bite. *Is something wrong?* Dad asks
for the second time. *No, nothing's wrong,* she says.

I'm not too hungry. That's all. Dad looks from her
to me, a question on his face. *Well*—he's trying
hard—*how are you two feeling about Pam and Blake
by now?* Abi looks like she might start crying,

but she doesn't want Dad to think she's having
a hard time about that. *Fine,* she says, and Dad
turns to me. *I like Blake,* I say, *but I miss Mom's
books and everything. I don't know why you had*

to get rid of everything. What did you do with them?
Dad looks surprised. *They're in boxes out in the shed.
I thought we could take them home when we leave.
Sorry, I didn't think about it. You should have said*

something. I don't know why he didn't think about it,
but at least he's listening now. I look down at my plate
and say, *It's okay.* We're all quiet for a few minutes. Then
Abi blurts out, *Dad, I thought things were going great,*

but what if I was wrong? Dad goes, *Huh?* And she takes
a deep breath and says, *See, there's this boy I kind of like, he's
cute and nice, and I thought he liked me—that's good, right?*
Dad says, *Right,* but he shakes his head. *Abi—please*

136

start from the beginning. When and where did you meet
this boy? Who is he? he asks. Abi says, *A few weeks*
ago. I can tell she's being careful not to say more
than she wants to. *I met him—Brock—at the beach.*

And now I think he likes someone else, and he didn't even
tell me why. I mean, I'm good enough—right? I'm not funny-
looking, am I? Dad gets that "Where's Pam when I
need her?" look, thinks for a minute, and says, *No, honey,*

never think that. You're perfect. He looks at me
and adds, *You both are.* That was nice of him.
You might think this boy is the best person in the world,
and I wish he thought the same about you. I'm

not so sure he doesn't, in fact. Sometimes you have to
talk to someone a little more. Get to know each
other. Take things one day at a time. One boy at a time.
He pats Abi's hand. She reaches for a piece

of pizza, takes a bite, does not look at me.
Dad says, *I'm glad we can talk about it.* Abi nods. *So*
am I, she says. Dad says, *Good.* Meaning: "The end."
If he only knew how much he doesn't know.

Later, as we're driving home, a few raindrops
hit the windshield. Then more. Then hail.

137

The wind picks up and Dad drives carefully, glancing at Abi and me, with a tight grip on the steering wheel.

Splashing Water on Blake's Hands
  The lake

After last night's storm,

people want to talk. They all come
out to see what the wind blew down.
Where are the swans? In the channel on my
eastern shore, their nest survived the storm. TJ
rowed in earlier, to check on them. Then he went

out with Devon and the twins, hoping to catch some
fish, but Sadie talked so much that TJ has turned back.

Blake is coming now. I'll meet him for the first time.
Usually, Claire and Abi run quickly down the path,
taking the stairs two at a time, but with the baby
they walk carefully. Down at the shore, the girls
enjoy splashing water on Blake's little hands.
Right when they're laughing together, the
four Johnsons go by. Sophia says, *TJ,*
look! The baby! Can we stop? TJ says
Yes, and pulls up to the dock.

One Boy at a Time
Abi

Everyone is crowding around Dad and Blake.
    When I step back so Devon can get a better look,
        TJ comes close to me and whispers, *Abi, do you*

want to see the swans? I rowed in early this morning
    and found their nest at the far end of the channel.
        I could take you to see them sometime if you want.

I've been thinking about what Dad said: *One boy*
    at a time. That would also mean one girl at a time,
        right? Apparently, Brock likes someone else, and

I do want to see the swans' nest. *Okay,* I whisper
    (because TJ whispered first). But why are we
        whispering? Who is not supposed to hear?

Maybe he doesn't want to take his little sisters
    and brother. Or maybe my sister? Claire would love
        to go along. But this is my first day not being grounded—

I can finally go where I want without her tagging along.
    Tomorrow morning? TJ suggests. I nod, and he says, *Let's meet*
        here at eight—he's still whispering. Claire gives us a funny look.

Nothing Much
  Claire

What were you and TJ whispering about?
I ask Abi, and she answers, *Nothing much.*
But then before we go to bed, she tells Dad, *I'm
going on a boat ride with TJ tomorrow.* Such

a small thing, maybe, but why didn't she tell me
when I asked her? Is there some reason they
don't want me to know? Am I now the person
Abi keeps her secrets from? Dad says, *Okay,*

*Abi. See if you can find out where he's
been catching all those fish! That boy sure
knows his way around this lake. And tell him
he'd be welcome to borrow my new lure.*

Does it occur to Dad that TJ is a boy
and Abi is a girl and they're going
out alone together? Or does he think, *It's only
TJ?* I guess Dad knows what he's doing.

Questions
Claire, kayaking to the beach

Abi left the house at eight. **Where**
       did she and TJ go, so secretly? **Does**
            it mean she likes TJ now in **this**
       new boy-girl way? Did they **leave**
the Johnson kids behind? Or just **me**?

I Leave That Out
Claire

I'm at the beach earlier than usual this morning
and I'm glad to see Jonilet. She's full of notes
and observations about what happened on the
two days Abi and I weren't here. *Two sailboats*

got so close to shore, the lifeguards had to close
the beach until the wind died down. Also, Brock
was here with that girl over there. She points
out the same girl who was with him on his dock

the other day. *I haven't seen her here before, but it seems*
like she knows Brock pretty well. Where's Abi today?
she asks. *She went on a boat ride,* I answer, *so I came*
by myself. She's not grounded anymore. I don't say

who she went on the boat ride with. I'm not sure
why I leave that out. So much depends
on what I don't know: Do Abi and TJ "like-like"
each other now, or are they still just friends?

A Quiet Place
Abi

TJ steers his little fishing boat
      up to the channel, then shuts
            off the motor and lets us drift

into the reeds. I take the oars and pull us
      to a quiet place I never knew was here.
            Finger to his lips, *Shhhh . . .* TJ points.

We sit in silence, watching a great white
      bird glide through the water toward a nest
            hidden in the reeds—and then the other swan

stands up in the nest, and turns, and settles back.
      Four eggs, TJ whispers. For a long time, we sit still
            in the boat, silently watching the pair of swans.

TJ turns and nods to me. *Let's see,* he whispers,
      if we can get a little closer. I row toward the nest
            without a sound. The swan lifts herself again,

nudges each egg with her beak. *Oh, TJ, look!*
      I whisper. The morning is so still, the two of us
            so quiet, we hear a tiny beak begin to crack its shell.

We watch until the baby swan is hatched.

    I release the breath I'm holding, and TJ turns

        to me, smiling, as the sun climbs into the sky.

We don't speak. Even when TJ motions me to lift

    the oars and row away, we hold our silence as we glide

        through the channel, back out on the lake. The motor,

when TJ starts it up again, seems quieter. We take

    the long way home. When we stop at my dock, TJ

        steadies the boat, and says, *Thanks, Abi,* as I step out.

Thank you, TJ, I reply. His smile comes from

    a warm, sun-bright place. After he goes home,

        I sit on the dock, my feet in the water, thinking, *I love*

the swans, I love TJ's smile, I love this lake . . . until

    the swans and the sun and the smile and the silence are

        impossible to separate, still and quiet, deep inside me.

Okay, I Can See That
Claire

When I get home I'm still annoyed that Abi and TJ
left me behind. I walk along the dock, and sit
down planning to tell Abi I saw Brock with that girl.
But there's something different about her, and it

makes me quiet. We listen to the lapping of small
waves on the shore. A school of minnows swims around
our feet. An eagle flies overhead, then dives
for a fish. Sitting here with Abi calms me down.

After a while, I ask: *Where did you and TJ go?*
Abi takes her time to answer. *We went to see
a swans' nest in the channel that leads to the next
lake over.* I look at her. *Why didn't you ask me*

to go along? There. I've asked. And Abi answers.
*I wasn't sure about that, Claire. I think TJ was trying
to slip away without the little kids finding out where
he was going or who he was going with.* Is she lying

so I won't feel bad? She goes on, *We had to
keep it quiet and he probably didn't want to worry*

146

about you and me talking the way we do, you know?
Okay, I can see that. I nod, and Abi says, *Sorry,*

though. You would have loved it. Maybe now that I
know where the swans are, we can take the canoe
and go see them. It's kind of far, but you've been
getting so strong this summer, I'm sure we could do

that now. We agree we'll get up early tomorrow
or the next clear morning and go out together.
Let's take oranges and hot chocolate, I suggest, *like Dad*
used to, when he took us fishing. I hope the weather

will cooperate—we only have one more week
before we leave. We sit for a while, dangling our feet.
Then Abi says, *I wish I knew what Brock is thinking.*
I tell her about seeing him. *You should go to the beach,*

I say. *Maybe he's embarrassed about being*
rescued the other night. He might want to talk
to you about that. If he's with that girl again,
you could just leave his clothes by his bike and walk

away before he sees you. When I think about that,
it seems kind of childish, but Abi listens to me,
nodding as if she's considering everything
I say. *I guess I could try asking him who he*

likes best—her or me, she says. *But then . . . what if he picks*
me, and it turns out I like . . . someone else better?
I don't answer that. Does she mean TJ? Probably.
This seems like something I should let her

figure out on her own. We dry our feet,
put our shoes on, and go back to the cabin.
Dad holds Blake's hand up in the air and says
in a squeaky baby voice, *Hi, Claire! Hi, Abi!*

A Fawn and Its Mother
Claire

I set my alarm last night before I went to bed
so I'd wake up early, like Abi does.
But it's the steady sound of a gentle rain
I'm hearing now, before the alarm goes

off. Which means no canoeing or early-morning
swim. That's okay. It turns out to be a good
day for all of us to stay inside together. I get out
our old Legos, and Abi asks, *Claire, would*

it be okay if I sketch you while you're putting
that spaceship together? Sure, that's fine—
why not? I don't pay much attention
until she finishes, and shows me her line

drawing. She's good. It looks a lot like me,
except she's done something to make my hair
look like it's pulled back from my face.
I ask, *What's that black thing right there?*

She reaches in her pocket and shows
me a hair clip like the one she's drawn,

then pushes back my bangs and puts it
in my hair. The rain has stopped. A fawn

steps out of the woods, and the mother
deer stands over it. The fawn starts to nuzzle
for its mother's milk. As I walk over to the window
to watch them, Pam looks up from the jigsaw puzzle

she's been working on and says, *That looks nice.*
She's talking about my hair, and Dad agrees.
While my whole family, even Blake, is looking
at me, the fawn disappears into the trees.

It Rises in the Yeast
Claire

After yesterday's rain, the air today is clear
and bright. Abi and I wake up early, and Dad
helps us make hot chocolate for our canoe trip.
As we walk down to the canoe, Abi says, *I've had*

Brock's clothes for six days now. I know—they're
still in the bag, at the back of our closet. *Maybe*
we should take them to the beach today, she says, *after*
we go to see the swans. I like that idea. Abi

and I start paddling east toward the sunrise,
remembering an old Dad-joke about east and west.
How is the sun like a loaf of bread? I ask, and Abi smiles
and answers, *It rises in the yeast, and sets behind your vest.*

My Form of Rest
The lake

I love these early-morning

hours when hardly anyone is up,
    everything calm on my surface, while below it's
all so full of life—underwater movement is my form of
rest. Yesterday was stormy, but now, here are these girls

    in their canoe, with hot chocolate and oranges.
        They're up early, out exploring.

    I recall the first time they tried canoeing—
neither of them could steer. Claire leaned over the edge,

tipping the canoe right over. Their father quickly rowed out to
help, but didn't tow them in. He calmly talked them through it, and
    eventually, they made it back to shore—laughing by then. Abi

    doesn't know that all the cygnets have hatched. Yesterday
    evening, they were tucked beneath their mother's wing
        enjoying a ride on her back. This morning, as a
        pink-and-orange sunrise streaks the sky, the girls

head toward the channel, slowing to watch an
egret fish in the shallows,
and the flock of
rooks fly from the rookery. Now
they have reached the channel, and the mother
swan swims toward them, as if to introduce her babies. She's

carrying three cygnets now—the fourth swims along beside her.
Oh, Abi whispers, as the swans glide past. Claire whispers back,
Remember the story of the ugly duckling? Baby swans are
even cuter than baby ducks, if you ask me.

Ring the Bell If You Need Me
Claire

We sit in our canoe watching the swans
for a long time. Then Abi says, *This is how
it was the other day with TJ. Neither of us wanted
to leave. It was quiet and peaceful, like it is now.*

When we're paddling back, the whole lake
seems like it's greeting us. Two beavers come
up close to our canoe. A dragonfly rides
on Abi's shoulder most of the way home.

Halfway up the path to the cabin, we meet
Pam walking down, carrying Blake
in a baby sling, all wrapped around her.
Claire, she says, *why don't you and I take*

*Blake down to the water for a few minutes. Abi—you
have a guest. A few minutes ago, there was a knock
at the front door, and a very nice young man
introduced himself. He said his name is Brock.*

Abi says, *You mean he's here—all by himself?*
I have to smile. Does she think he'd bring

his new girlfriend along, or what? *Yes, he is,*
Pam says. I can see Abi's thoughts swing

back and forth as she looks from Pam to me.
Should she say, *Come on, Claire—you come, too?*
Or not? She settles on "not," takes a deep breath,
and turns toward the cabin. *Ring the bell if you*

need me, I sort of joke. We haven't used that bell
since we were too little to tell time, and Dad
would ring it to call us in for meals. We knew
exactly where our boundaries were—we had

to stay between the driveway and the row
of pine trees; we couldn't go near the road. We
wore whistles around our necks, so if we did
get lost, we could whistle for Dad and he

would come and find us. I wonder if Abi
ever misses those days, like I sometimes do.
Pam looks at Blake, then at me, studying our faces.
You know, Claire, she says, *he looks a lot like you.*

I look at him to see if I can see what Pam sees, and
that poem comes into my mind. *Hey, Tyger,* I whisper,
kissing him on the top of his head. *What a*
great nickname, Pam says. *If your dad and sister*

like it, too, maybe we should call him that, at least
while he's a baby. When he gets a little older,
he can tell us what to call him, like Abi has.
Pam likes my idea? I'm glad I told her.

More Lemonade?
   Abi

I find Brock sitting on the porch.

      Pam gave him a glass of lemonade,

            and put one on the table for me, too.

We both start talking at the same time,

      saying the exact same thing: *Umm . . .*

            and then we both stop and wait,

hoping the other will speak first. *Here's your hoodie,*

      he finally says. *Oh, thanks,* I say. *And you left your*

            shoes and clothes on our dock. I was bringing them

to you the other day, but then . . . Never mind, I'll be right back.

      I get his clothes and give them to him. *Thanks,* he says,

            then, *Why did you and your sister turn your canoe around*

instead of paddling over so I could introduce you to Rachel?

      How am I supposed to answer that? *I don't know,* I say.

            Awkward silence. *Do you want some more lemonade?*

I wish Pam and Claire would come back. *No thanks,*

      says Brock. *I'm good. I should go. My cousins are leaving*

            this afternoon. I didn't know his cousins were— Wait.

Is Rachel . . . your cousin? I ask. He gives me a funny look.

    Yeah, he says. *They come every summer for about a week.*

        She's my age, almost like a sister. We get along great.

I try to act like: Oh. Right. I knew that.

    But my face gives me away. *Abi,* Brock asks,

        did you think . . . ? I start to say, *It looked like . . .*

But I'm not sure what it did look like. I

    didn't stop to look. *Brock,* I ask, *what did you*

        think, when Claire and I turned the canoe around

like that? I think he blushes as he answers,

    I thought you didn't like me so much anymore, after

        you found out I couldn't swim as far as you. That was

horrible—your little sister rescuing me, and all.

    I hadn't thought of it from his point of view. I don't

        want him to think that's true. *No, I still like you, Brock,*

I say. Then he smiles, and I smile, and we laugh

    a little bit. He puts his arm around me, tries

        to pull me close—I'm not sure why I turn away.

An Idea for Pam
Claire

As Pam and I walk along the lakeshore, she
picks up a pinecone and says, *Maybe I could
do some "Pointers" about this for my blog. How
could this be used?* I have an idea: the wood-

stove is sometimes hard to start—I look at
all the pinecones on the ground: *Dip them
in candle wax and use them for fire starters?*
When I see how easy it is to make Pam

happy I feel a little guilty for not trying to do it
before now. *Yes!* she says. (Is this even an original
idea? I might have seen it online somewhere.)
I think harder—"Pointers from Pam" in its final

form has to be more elaborate. *Maybe,* I say, *you
could add glitter to the wax, so it would be a table
decoration before you use it for the fire.* Pam looks
surprised. Does she think I'm not capable

of having ideas? Or—this would be worse—is she
surprised to be having a friendly conversation

with me? *Thank you, Claire,* she says. Maybe Pam
and I could just enjoy what's left of our vacation.

The Truth Starts Pounding
Abi

I wish I had an answer when Brock asks,

    Why? I told him I still like him—and he

        still likes me. We both enjoy kissing.

So it must be confusing when I turn away.

    I try to explain: *When I thought you liked another*

        girl, I felt bad. And I don't want you to feel like that

if I like someone else sometime. Not that I do, but . . .

    I stop, because I'm trying to tell the truth, and I

        might be starting not to. Brock waits for me to finish.

This is way harder than I thought it would be. *Abi,*

    he says, *I like you for a lot of reasons. You're really fun.*

        You're smart. You're pretty. And, boy, can you swim.

It's my turn to say something. But when I try,

    the truth starts pounding in my ear. I can't say:

        I do like you, Brock. It's just that I like TJ more.

For a second, I'm tempted to kiss him

    in order to fill this awkward silence. I don't

        want to hurt his feelings. I don't want to lie.

But I don't want to kiss him, either. I take a deep breath
      and say the best thing I can think of: *Would it be okay*
            if we just like each other . . . but don't kiss anymore?

He steps away from me. Stops smiling. Stands
      on one foot, then the other. *I guess so,* he finally says,
            (What else can he say?) *but I still don't understand why.*

Claire and Pam are coming up the path. I say, *Thanks*
      for bringing back my hoodie. Brock says, *Thanks for these.*
            He picks up his shoes and clothes. And then he leaves.

How Should We Celebrate?
Claire

Abi is very quiet after Brock leaves.
Not sad. Not happy either. More like
she's thinking about something. She
goes off by herself for a long bike

ride, and while she's gone, Dad says, *Claire,*
I can hardly believe that you will be eleven
in two days. How should we celebrate this year?
I've thought about this. *The year I was seven,*

I say, *we had the Johnsons over for a cookout,*
remember? And we made strawberry ice cream
for dessert. Can we do that again? Dad says,
I remember that night—the girls' team

beat the boys' team in Frisbee keep-away. Maybe
we should wait a few years before we try that again.
Let Blake get big enough to give us some backup
if the twins sit on the Frisbee, like they did back then.

Later, after dinner, Pam calls Mrs. Johnson,
and they agree they'll all come over in two

days. Abi offers to help Pam make my cake.
Thanks, Abi, I whisper. *I can count on you*

to be sure it's chocolate marble—Pam might
think carrot cake is healthier. I don't know
how Abi feels about us inviting TJ's family.
She doesn't say anything about it, so

it must be okay. At sunset, Dad wraps Blake
in the baby sling, and he and Pam go for a walk.
As soon as we're alone, Abi says, *Claire, can we*
talk about what happened this afternoon, with Brock?

My sister wants to talk to me about her love life.
It's weird, but for some reason I've kind
of gotten interested. We sit on the porch while
Abi talks nonstop. About boys. And—I don't mind.

I Close My Eyes
Claire

I've had a good day, but I can't get to sleep.
Too much to think about: What is kissing
like? What if you hurt someone's feelings?
(Or they might hurt yours.) Why am I missing

Mom so much, even though I hardly knew her?
I close my eyes, and she starts to appear
as if in a dream, and then she comes closer, like
she's saying, *Claire, it's okay.* The mother deer

I saw with her fawn the other day steps into
my mind. The swans. A dragonfly. The leap
of a fish, only without a splash, just endless
circles going toward shore as I fall asleep.

If I'm Going to Try
Claire

Abi wakes up for her morning swim
and shakes me out of my dreams.
Want to swim to the island and back? she asks.
We'll be leaving in four days, which means

if I'm going to try, I'd better do it now.
Okay, I say. *I hope TJ is up. He said he'd row
along beside me.* Abi says, *I don't think you need
his help, but we can ask.* That was an hour ago,

and now here I am, feeling strong and happy,
taking these last few strokes as we arrive
at Anna's Island. I stand on the shore and wave
to TJ in his boat, then turn to Abi for a high five!

I rest awhile before going back in the water. Will I
be able to swim back, against the current? *I want
to do this while I'm still ten,* I say as I start out. Abi says,
You will, Claire. TJ calls, *Remember, if you can't—*

Abi interrupts him. *No, forget that. Let's go.*
We step into the water together, and I swim

all the way home—with no help! I'm glad TJ was
with us all the way, even though I didn't need him.

That Boy You Mentioned
Claire

Dad can be a few steps behind, but he always
catches up eventually. Today, he's cooking
scrambled eggs for lunch, and says to Abi,
You know that boy you mentioned—I'm looking

forward to meeting him. Abi has to think a minute
to remember that she told Dad about Brock
the other day. *Oh. Yes. That boy,* she says. *Well,*
you might not actually meet him. Dad gets this look

that means he realizes he missed something,
and Abi takes pity on him, answering the question
he doesn't ask. *We're still friends—I think—but no more*
than that. Pam looks up and offers a suggestion:

Maybe, she says, *you should talk to him one more*
time before you leave, to say goodbye. Just so you end
the summer on a good note. That way, when we come
back next summer, you'll still have him as a friend.

I notice that Pam says "when we come back."
We—she understands that she belongs here.

I look more closely at what she's doing—
dipping pinecones in candle wax. Where

did she get those half-burned candles to melt? A box
on the table says "Cari's candles" in Dad's writing.
Dad and I went out to the shed yesterday and
brought in some boxes. Just a few. Not everything.

I hand Pam a jar of glitter to sprinkle on a warm,
wax-dipped pinecone. *Thanks,* she says. *Do you want
to help?* Sure—why not? I look around the cabin.
Blake's (Tyger's) things are scattered around. A plant

Pam brought home the other day is blooming on
a shelf they emptied. Dad told Abi and me to take
what we wanted of Mom's to our room. A few books.
Her red sandals. Her painting of a sunset on the lake.

A Haircut and a Kiss
Claire

Ever since Abi drew that picture, and gave me
her hair clip, I've been using it in my hair. Now
I decide to cut my bangs. I get a pair of scissors
and hold a chunk of hair, just above my eyebrow.

But when I cut it off, and then another, I look
nothing like I thought I would. How do you cut
your own hair, anyway? When I see myself
in the mirror, it seems like it will be easy, but

it definitely is not. There's this zigzag line
across my forehead, and not enough hair
left to make it straight. What should I do?
Forget it—I'll leave it this way. I don't care.

I pull my cap down over my face, but I must
have a funny expression, because Pam says, *What*
happened? She gently lifts my cap to look
at me. She doesn't laugh. I appreciate that.

I can fix this, she says. Not too long ago
I might have stomped off and told her

I did not need fixing, but today I say, *Really?*
She says, *Sure. On my laptop, I have a folder*

full of pictures of girls' hairstyles. Have a look,
and see what you like. She doesn't hover
over me, she just studies the picture I find,
gets a hand-mirror, and a towel to put over

my shoulders, and then *snip, snip, snip,*
and she's done. Dad says, *You look more*
like an eleven-year-old this way. Pam shakes the
towel outside. I sweep the hair up off the floor.

Just as good as Chloe, Abi says. Pam takes my chin
in her hand, tilts back my head. I don't squirm away.
She smiles, admiring her handiwork, then leans in
to kiss my forehead. I have to admit, I look okay.

Eleven
Claire

Happy Birthday, Abi says, as soon as we wake up.
Then, early afternoon: *Are you going to the beach?*
Jonilet might be there, and I bet she's wondering
where you've been. It's not hard for me to reach

two conclusions: Pam and Abi are planning
to make my birthday cake—they've agreed
it's Abi's job to get me out of the way. And
Abi isn't going to the beach herself, but she'd

love to know if Brock is there and, if so, whether
he's sad and lonely—or not. *Yes, I'm going,* I say.
I head out in the kayak, paddling through
the water lilies, counting by elevens all the way.

I pass eleven docks, and see eleven ducks.
Eleven puffy clouds roam the clear blue sky.
They seem to float in front of me as I cut
through the water. When I get to the beach, I

pull the kayak out and count some more:
Eleven teenagers in the group Abi usually

sits with—two girls wave to me as I walk past.
Brock sees me and looks a little bit confused.

Maybe he's wondering where Abi is.
Trinity walks over from the concession stand
with an ice cream cone she gives to him.
Good, there's Jonilet. She waves, and

calls out, *Claire—Happy Birthday! Sit with me.* Wow,
she remembers my birthday from last summer. *Hey,*
she says, *we're the same age again. What's different
about you?* I shrug. *Your hair,* she says. *I like it that way.*

Benjamin Bunny
Abi

From what Claire says, it sounds like Pam is right
        that I should try to talk to Brock before we leave.
                He might still be thinking he did something

that made me not like him anymore. Which isn't true,
        but I don't know what more to say, or how to say it.
                Now Claire is sitting on her bed across from me,

holding Benjamin Bunny and lecturing: *I still say*
        you should give him back to TJ. (Does TJ remember
                giving him to me?) *I have an idea,* says Claire.

When they come over tonight, why don't you
        leave Benjamin Bunny out on a chair and see what
                happens. If TJ doesn't remember, he won't even notice,

and if he does, you can give him back. It's logical enough,
        but there's something I can't admit to Claire. After all
                these years, I'm not sure I want to give this bunny back.

Abi and TJ Sitting in a Tree
Claire

It's crowded in our cabin with the whole
Johnson family plus the five of us. Devon
and the twins start to squish onto a narrow
bench on one side of the table, but then, even

though there are enough chairs for the rest
of us, Abi and TJ offer to take the bench. It's
so obvious. Sadie and Sophia start singing
that song: *Abi and TJ sitting in a tree, K-I-S—*

But before TJ has a chance to stop them, Dad
interrupts, *What is it with children's songs and trees
anyway—that one, and the other one about a cradle
with a baby in it, falling down from a treetop? These*

*days, would anyone really rock a baby in a treetop?
Or sit in a tree kissing, for that matter?* By the time
he's said all that, nobody's paying any attention
to how close together Abi and TJ are sitting. I'm

telling Devon where everything is on the table
so he can help himself, as Sadie and Sophia try

to get ketchup on their hot dogs, while Mom and
Mrs. Johnson are— Whoa, stop right there. Did I

just say "Mom" when I meant Pam? Not out loud,
but still. I want to think about that a little more.
After we eat, Dad and Mr. Johnson suggest
a Frisbee game, and we all head out the door,

trying to decide if boys-against-girls would be fair
this year. As TJ goes out the door, I see him pause
to pick up Benjamin Bunny from the chair that
Abi sat him in. *Abi, you still have this? Because*

I was thinking, we could give it to Blake—or should
I say Tyger? Funny, I thought it had more hair.
Abi laughs. *I guess I kind of wore that off*
when I was little. He does look kind of threadbare,

doesn't he? She says "he" and TJ says "it."
TJ doesn't care about this, and he knows Abi
will enjoy sharing Benjamin Bunny with Tyger.
So that's all settled. After we play Frisbee,

we make strawberry ice cream to go with the
chocolate-marble birthday cake Pam and Abi made.
We build a fire on the beach and sit around it,
talking, remembering other times we've played

Frisbee on people's birthdays. Dad asks, *What will
we all remember about this summer, after we've gone
home?* Abi and I look at each other, thinking of things
we won't say, but she does say, *I'll never forget the swan*

and her cygnets coming out of the channel. She lets
it be known that TJ showed them to her, and once
the twins hear that, it's: *When did you go? How come
you didn't take us? We want to see the swans!*

What a commotion. I tell them, *This is why you two
can't go. When you get near the swans, you have to be
quiet or you'll scare the babies.* Devon pipes up,
I can be quiet. Can I go? Abi and TJ look at me,

and we nod to each other. We could take Devon.
The twins start yelling, *No fair! We can be quiet, too!*
We laugh at them, and they get the joke and
quiet down. *Promise,* Sadie whispers. One canoe

could hold four people, but not six. We make a plan:
TJ and Devon can take Sadie in their canoe, and Abi
and I can take Sophia in ours. Sadie gloats,
Sophia and I can go, but not Tyger. He's a noisy baby.

See You Next Summer, Maybe
Abi

Okay, I know I have to talk to Brock. I owe him
        some kind of explanation—as honest as I can be
                without hurting his feelings too much. This is

when he usually goes running—I'm headed his way,
        hoping (kind of) to see him. Sure enough, there he is—
                he waves and slows down a little, lets me catch up.

We run together for a few minutes without talking,
        then stop at a drinking fountain with a bench beside it.
                I want to get this over with—I sit down, and Brock sits

beside me. I wish I knew how to begin. Then, before
        I say anything, he starts the conversation: *Abi,* he says,
                I don't want to hurt your feelings, but— What? I was not

expecting this—*you'll be leaving in a couple days,*
        and I'll still be here. I think Trinity might like me,
                so . . . He looks at me with a question on his face.

Oh. That's okay, I say. *I understand.* He looks surprised.
        You do? he says. I nod. Somehow, we've each said exactly
                the right words, and no more. How did we figure this out?

Friends? he asks, putting up his hand for a fist-bump. I answer,

Sure. Bye. See you next summer, maybe. Is this how Claire felt

the other day, when she swam home from Anna's Island?

The Swans Swim Closer
Claire

Midafternoon, Abi and I paddle to TJ's dock
and get Sophia settled in the center
of our canoe. Devon and TJ, with Sadie,
lead the way across the lake. After we enter

the channel we stay together as we get closer
to the swans—the twins are ready to explode
from the effort of keeping quiet. *Is this
exactly where you were when TJ showed*

you the baby swans? Sophia whispers.
Abi points, *No, they were right over there.*
We paddle carefully that way, but stop
before we get to the nest so we don't scare

them. TJ brings his canoe beside ours
and reaches out to take Abi's hand,
pulling our two canoes together. Sadie
and Sophia hold hands, too, and

I glance over at Devon to see if he wants
to help, but he's facing the other way.

Plus, he's nine, and probably thinks
girls have cooties—which is okay

with me. We stay together for a while. Then
Abi and TJ drop hands so they can steer.
In this almost perfect silence, Devon picks up
some small sound that none of us can hear

and points in a direction we weren't
looking. Sadie lets out a squeak of delight,
then claps both hands over her mouth
as the whole swan family—the two white

parents and four gray balls of fluff—come
into view. Sophia is so quiet, I glance
back to make sure she's okay. She whispers,
Claire, I never thought we'd get a chance

to be this close to them. The swans swim over
to where we float in our canoes. No one speaks—we
don't need to. It's like we're all one person. One
heart beating. At least that's how it feels to me.

This Day
Abi

I love everything about this day.
  The swan family, our two canoes
    coming home late in the afternoon,

Devon offering to put their life vests away
  and take the tired twins back to the house.
    And Claire paddling our canoe home

by herself without saying why. She knows
  TJ and I want to be alone for a little while,
    to say goodbye. She guesses that we'll kiss.

When we do, it's different from last year.
  A thousand memories, a million maybes,
    a flash of joy—like lightning, only softer.

Heartstones
The lake

One more day

before they leave. Ah, a heart-shaped
red stone—let me move it close to shore.
Abi's head is in the clouds today, but
Claire sees the stone right at the
edge of my water, and

stoops to pick it up. She
turns it, admiring its lines and colors.
Eleven years I've known her—from baby, to
rambunctious toddler, to this strong young girl
now beginning to consider the possibility that
even she might want to kiss someone—not
right away but, maybe, someday?

Today she's content to find and
hold this stone. She lifts it to the sun to let it dry,
and dips it back into the water. After she does that several
times, she puts it in her pocket so she can take it home. Every

summer, she searches for a perfect stone, and often finds one on
the last afternoon before they go back home. I'll always
remember the words she said the first time she found
a heartstone and proudly showed it to her dad:
Is this from Mom? Since then, I always try to
nudge one to shore for her to find.

Until We Come Back
Claire

I show Dad and Pam the heartstone I found this afternoon,
and Dad gives me a hug. I'm superstitious about this now:
It brings me luck until we come back next year, I explain to Pam.
She turns the stone over in her hand, thoughtful. *Is that how*

the lake got its name? she asks. *Yes,* I say. *I find a heartstone
every year. You've seen them, in my room at home, in a bird's-nest
I keep on my dresser. Dad says heartstones are a sign of love—
we should find one for you.* Abi jumps up, missing the rest

of the conversation as she bounces out the door. I bet she's
going down to the lake to look for one to give to TJ.
Sure enough, she's gone for over an hour, and comes back
smiling. *I found a heartstone,* she announces, *and gave it away*

(to TJ of course), *and then TJ gave this one to me!*
Dad, she asks, *when will we be coming back to close
the cabin this year?* Dad laughs—Abi and I usually
hate that weekend, and from her expression, he knows

she's looking forward to it. *Sometime around Halloween,
as usual,* he says, and then he adds, just to tease

her, *You could stay home this year if you don't want to help.*
She says, *No, we'll come. Right, Claire?* And then, *Please,*

Dad, could we come up for Thanksgiving and Christmas, too?
I want to see what winter is like up here. Dad says, *It's cold!*
But he adds, *We'll see. I've been thinking we should*
winterize this place pretty soon—before I get too old

to do the work. I think he's joking about that—he'll be
young for a long time—but it makes me wonder
if Abi and I will still be coming up here years from now
when Dad *is* old. Our babies crawling around under

the table, Abi and I and TJ and Devon and the twins
all grown up. Tyger and the Johnsons' new baby
might be the age we are now. Dad interrupts this
line of thought with a reminder: *Claire and Abi,*

when your own things are packed, could you help
clean up the kitchen and get things in the car?
We go in our room and pack things in boxes, to stay
here, or in suitcases, to go home. Abi picks up the jar

of rice and fishes out her phone. *I guess I'll*
have to tell Dad my phone went for a swim,
she says. She gave up on it about a week ago,
but she tries once more. *I wish I didn't have to tell him*

about that, she says. *I hope he'll get me a new one.* She points
the phone at me, something clicks, and she waves it in the air.
Look! she says. *The rice dried it out—at least the camera
works.* Abi-luck strikes again. In the picture, my hair

looks different than I'm used to, but I don't hate it.
Which really means, I have to admit, I don't hate Pam.
If she's not too busy being Tyger's mom to make time for me
and Abi, and if she wonders if I'm ready to accept that—I am.

As for Abi—when I saw her start to change so much,
I missed her. I felt like she was leaving me behind.
But it's interesting to see where she's going, and if I
ever head down that path, I won't be traveling blind.

After we get our room packed, I ask Pam if she needs
help in the kitchen, and she says, *Thanks, Claire. I sure do.*
I can't get anything done while Tyger needs all my attention.
Could you try to keep him occupied for half an hour or so?

And that's how I come to fall in love a little bit myself.
Pam wraps him around me in the baby sling and we
go down to the lake. A great blue heron flies overhead,
I smile down at Tyger—and he smiles back at me.

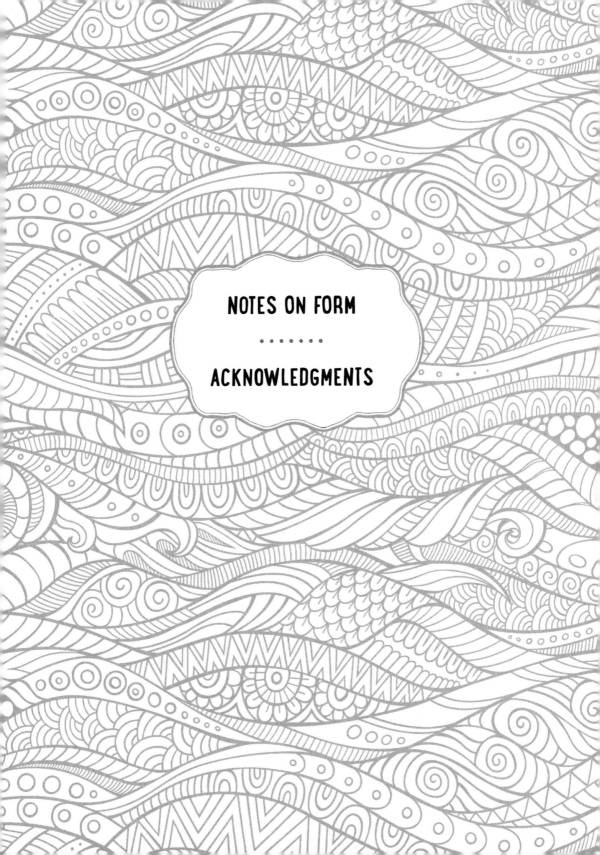

NOTES ON FORM

· · · · · · ·

ACKNOWLEDGMENTS

NOTES ON FORM

AS YOU MAY HAVE NOTICED, the poems in *When My Sister Started Kissing* are written in different forms.

Most of Claire's poems are in quatrains (four-line stanzas) with the second and fourth lines rhyming, sometimes with a half-rhyme or a light rhyme (just one sound matching in the words at the ends of those two lines).

In Claire's kayak poems, to create the sensation of the kayak moving through water, I've set the words at the ends of the lines in boldface; these words say more about what is on Claire's mind.

Abi's poems are in a free-verse form, shaped on the page in jagged three-line stanzas, to resemble lightning.

The poems in the voice of the lake are acrostics: the first letters of each line, when read down the left side of the page, spell something out—this is called the armature of the acrostic. In these lake poems, I have used lines from poems I love as the armatures. They represent the current running through the lake.

Here are the poems from which I have taken these lines:

Pages 3–4   "Tyger Tyger, burning bright,"
                     From "The Tyger," by William Blake

Page 18   "Somebody loves us all."
                     From "The Filling Station," by Elizabeth Bishop

Pages 45–46   ". . . lie back, and the sea will hold you."
                     From "First Lesson," by Philip Booth

Pages 74–75   "Live not for the-end-of-the-song / Live in the along."
                     From "Speech to the Young. Speech to the
                     Progress-Toward," by Gwendolyn Brooks

Pages 80–81   "She folds her wings about her sleeping child."
                     From "Bats," by Randall Jarrell

Pages 101–102   "Life is what it is about;"
                     From "Keeping Quiet," by Pablo Neruda
                     (Alastair Reid, translator)

Pages 119–120   "What can anyone give you greater than now,"
                     From "You Reading This, Be Ready," by William Stafford

Page 139   "A power of Butterfly . . ."
                     From "From the Chrysalis," by Emily Dickinson

Pages 152–153   "I hear it in the deep heart's core."

From "The Lake Isle of Innisfree," by William Butler Yeats

Pages 183–184   ". . . O brace sterner that strain!"

From "The Handsome Heart," by Gerard Manley Hopkins

ACKNOWLEDGMENTS

THANKS TO Margaret Ferguson, my editor, and to Susan Dobinick, Karla Reganold, and so many others at FSG who bring this book from my hands to yours. All we learned from Frances Foster shines through these pages.

Thanks to the young readers I meet in schools—I couldn't include all of your names, but I hear your strong, clear voices as I write.

Thanks to writer friends and teachers and reviewers and librarians—we are lucky in the community we create and sustain. Special thanks to Ginger Knowlton and Kate Kubert Puls.

Thanks to early readers, especially the Fort Wayne SCBWI group, Ruth Kronlokken, Ingrid Wendt, and young readers Jem and Naima van Tyn, Christine Howe, Gemma Goette, and fifth-grade students at Rick Marcotte Central School in South Burlington, Vermont—and to their parents and teachers.

I thank my children, Lloyd and Glen, and my large extended family. I believe David Kronlokken is to be credited with the peanut butter ravioli recipe.

Again and always, love and thanks to Chad.